CAROL OLSEN M.A.

Illustrated By

Student Artists

Gig Harbor Press
Gig Harbor, Washington

Publisher's Cataloging in Publication
(Prepared by Quality Books Inc.)

Olsen, Carol
    Left-over Louie / by Carol Olsen; illustrated by student
artists.
        p. cm.
        LCCN 93-070049
        ISBN 1-883078-75-X (Hdbk.)   ISBN 1-883078-76-8 (Pbk.)
        Audience: Ages 7-11, grades 2-6.
        SUMMARY: Louie Twitwhistle, a fifth-grader in the Northwest, is
challenged by his teacher to be himself. For Louie that means
accepting his shortcomings and developing his gifts.
        1. Self-realization--Juvenile fiction. 2. Self-perception in adolescents--Juvenile
fiction.   I. Title.

PZ7.O574Lef 1992   [Fic]
                                          QBI93-20020
                10   9   8   7   6   5   4   3   2

For my father, my brother, and all other

"Louies" who dare to be different

Thank you to my sons, Jeff and Greg, who listened to many story revisions; to my husband Bob, who tirelessly helped with publication; to my sister Miriam for her encouragement; to my students, past and present, whose imagination inspired the illustrations; to my mother who nurtured my creativity and modeled the joy of teaching; to Les Garcia, whose artistic vision led to the selection of students as illustrators, and to my lifelong friend, Janet, who made the book a reality.

Contents

ILLUSTRATIONS

Before the Story

Mrs. Butterhorn taught the fifth grade Discovery program for Coastline School District. She was noted for saying, "Always be yourself." She had a way of making each of her students feel special. To spotlight their uniqueness, she found contests for them to enter. Kids in her class won top awards in the Tansy Ragwort Weed Control Contest, sponsored by the County Committee Against Obnoxious Weeds. Their winning art work appeared on bookmarks, T-shirts, and even billboards. Their posters taught the world important stuff like: "Feed Your Aardvark"; "Adopt a Raincloud"; and "Say No to Everything But Homework." They even won a personal invitation to the twenty-fifth birthday of a Silverback gorilla.

They weren't surprised when Mrs. Butterhorn hit them with the news. A publishing company was sponsoring a "Win an Author" contest. To win, the class had to suggest a character for a new book. First prize was a visit from the author.

America is a melting pot. Harmony Harbor Elementary was a potluck of personalities, and Mrs. Butterhorn's class for gifted kids was a smorgasbord of eccentrics. One stood out like a main entré. His parents named him Louis, pronounced "Louie," like the French kings, but the kids had other names for him.

Mrs. Butterhorn's class wrote an essay describing Louie. They won first place in the nation. The author visited Harmony Harbor, where she met Louie and many other characters. Here is her story.

Carol Olsen

1 Pen War

It was a typical rainy Friday afternoon in Harmony Harbor. The students in Catherine Butterhorn's 5th grade class began to clean out their desks. Mrs. Butterhorn usually allowed fifteen minutes, which gave most of the students plenty of time to organize their supplies. Kara Suko began sorting her felt pens, papers, books, novelty erasers, pencils . . . .

Then she heard Mrs. Butterhorn say, "Today, boys and girls, I want you to empty your desks completely for a thorough cleaning."

"What?" It seemed like a waste of time to Kara, whose desk was in near perfect order. However, she obediently began to remove items from her desk, one at a time.

3

Then a voice with a slow Southern accent came over the intercom. It was Mr. Gritz, the principal. "Please don't be alarmed," he drawled. "This is a test of the school broadcasting system. I am conducting an earthquake drill. Y'all take your places as though you were experiencing a real earthquake. I repeat, this is only a test." A flurry of activity drowned out his last words.

Everyone ducked under their desks. Even Mrs. Butterhorn crawled under hers. They grabbed the legs of their desks. That was to keep the furniture from moving in case of a real earthquake.

Then it hit! The floor shook. Books scattered. Felt pen missiles flew through the air!

"What is it?" Kara panicked. "Another volcano erupting? Tentacles of an earthquake reaching into the Northwest? Nuclear holocaust? Wait a minute. The announcement said, 'This is only a test.'"

When the shaking stopped, she peered over the rubble. Her desk lay on its side. The legs of the desk on her left pointed straight into the air. The upturned desk belonged to the infamous Louie Twitwhistle.

Louie had been in Kara's class every year since kindergarten. "He's weird," she told everyone. "Everything about him is different, even his name. Who ever heard of Twitwhistle? He has disgusting habits like blowing his nose on his sleeve. He doesn't wear a belt. When he bends over everyone can see his underwear. He's totally unathletic. Every teacher in the school works on him. He's like a group project. Talking is the only thing he does well, but I can't understand him because he talks funny. I don't know what he's doing in Mrs. Butterhorn's class. She's supposed to have the smart kids."

A familiar voice called, "Watch out for the pyroclastic flow!"

Taking a slow, deep breath, Kara got up on her knees, her chest rising, her face expanding with the force of air against pinched lips. Her entire life force funneled through narrow, cold, black slits, as she glared at Louie Twitwhistle. His eyebrows arched and his pupils opened. "It's the harmonic tremors. They'll get you every time," he explained with his dry British wit.

"Harmonic tremors'll get you every time."

A voice swelled up inside Kara and burst forth, breaking the silence, "Louie!" Thirty-two heads turned in one motion, as though choreographed for a Broadway musical. Louie drew back into a tight little ball and covered his head with his arms.

Mrs. Butterhorn left the safety of her desk to check on the disturbance. She gazed down into Kara's stunned face. Kara closed her mouth to catch her breath. She braced herself for the aftermath--the lecture on "overreacting." She knew it was coming. It wasn't the first time she'd heard it. Mrs. Butterhorn didn't understand how it was living with Louie. He had brought this disaster down on both of them.

Bored with the earthquake drill, Louie shook the legs of his desk to imitate a real quake. He dumped his desk along with hers, emptying the contents in a heap at their feet. It was a case of order versus chaos. Like plates in the earth's crust, the two desks collided.

"It's Louie's fault!" Kara cried.

Louie dug frantically through the pile. Kara shouted, "What are you doing?"

"Looking for the fault line!" Louie squealed with delight.

"Stop that! You're mixing my stuff in with yours."

"I'd like to measure your reaction on the Richter Scale," Louie teased.

Kara dug through the pile, pulling her possessions protectively in her direction. She extracted her math book out from under crumpled, coffee stained, half finished assignments. She fished pencils out of a sticky glob of rubber cement. Kara disengaged her spiral notebook from the fuselage of a broken World War I biplane model. Her notebook fell open to her last journal entry. She read it to herself.

Date-September 22

Assignment: A Study in Contrasts

    I like order, It's in my blood. I get up every morning at exactly 6:00 A.M. I eat a balanced breakfast of oatmeal, toast, and orange juice. My lunch goes in a crisp white paper bag, labeled with my name. I include something from each major food group, using whole grain bread and avoiding granulated sugar. For exercise, I do some ballet stretches. I practice the piano without being asked. My backpack holds the things I'll need for the day such as notes for field trips, absences, fund raisers, or class pictures. My life is as tight and orderly as a zippered sandwich bag. I give my hair a final brush and double check to see that everything matches from my shoes to my hair ornaments. I view the world clearly through untinted contact lenses.

Then, there's Louie. He thrives on chaos. His hair hangs in a disorderly way around his shoulders. He looks like he's been on an extended camping trip with no running water. He wears a flannel shirt in any weather and baggy jeans with no belt. His pant legs drag on the floor. Shuffling into the classroom at the last possible minute, he carries his recycled brown bag lunch in a faded blue duffel bag. Louie too, is a creature of habit. Bad habit. Each day for lunch he has a thermos of coffee with cream and a powdered sugar donut. That is, unless he sets his duffel bag down too hard and breaks the liner in his

thermos. Then he just has a donut
and a big mess.

As she put away her journal Kara thought,
"Mrs. Butterhorn should be thrilled to have a
student like me. I am a teacher's dream--hard
working, immaculate--not to mention brilliant.
Yet, somehow she seems to favor Louie." She
wrinkled her forehead and frowned in Louie's
direction.

Kara put the lid back on her rubber cement.
"I remember the day he brought in that old musty
blue bottle. He said he dug it up in his back
yard. He gave it to Mrs. Butterhorn as a gift.
Can you imagine? It was filthy dirty and smelled
bad. I know teachers have to be polite. I figured
she threw it away in the faculty room trash can.
But no--The next day I saw it on her desk with
flowers in it. For the next week we had an
archaeology theme. We did our math on an
abacus and spelled words like 'artifact' and
'preserve.' Mrs. Butterhorn taught a history
lesson on the Clovis point arrowheads that were

recently found in the eastern part of our state. We even sang a song about bones. We did all of this because of Louie. He dragged in all the trash he had dug up in his back yard. He brought more smelly bottles, musty newspapers, and bragged for weeks about a gold ring he dug up and then accidentally lost. Did he really expect us to believe that his magpie stole it?"

She sneezed. "Or, how about the week he was absent with allergy problems and Mrs. Butterhorn bought that stuffed penguin for him at a thrift shop. If I hear once more about his penguin collection or his plans to be an Antarctic explorer, I'm going to puke in living color. It was so humiliating sitting next to a used penguin all week. Everyone knows a person with allergy problems should be dust-proofing, not dust-collecting." She coughed. Kara's eyes widened, her eyebrows arched, the color left her cheeks. "I hope the old saying's not true that 'Opposites attract!'"

Recess and half the math period passed before Kara could restore order. She was just finishing a quick inventory of her school supplies when Mrs. Butterhorn asked her to get back to work. Louie had somehow managed to stuff almost everything back in his desk.

Kara looked over at Louie. He was doing his math with a pen. Mrs. Butterhorn never allowed her students to work math problems in pen. Kara raised her hand to inform Mrs. Butterhorn about Louie's latest, disregard for rules when she discovered something familiar about the black pen Louie was using. She bent over to get a closer look. By straining her eyes she could just barely read the inscription, "Micro-Fine U.S.A." Why, that was her new erasable pen. "The little creep is using my pen," she boiled. Mrs. Butterhorn was busy on the other side of the room. "I can take care of this," she thought. She reached across Louie's desk and grabbed the pen. I guess she startled him or something. A loud cry and a deafening roar broke the silence. A violent force pulled Kara's body toward Louie. Gripping the pen and wrapping her feet around the legs of her desk, she tried desperately to resist the force. The next thing she knew she was lying next to Louie, buried under a very familiar pile of rubble. She pulled an empty hand out of a sticky puddle of goo.

"I told you to watch out for the pyroclastic flow," a knowing voice spoke. Louie smiled, waving the pen like a sword. His eyes sparkled as he announced, "No math today. Saved by the Pen War."

Kara cleaned up her mess first and Louie noticed that she was writing something on a piece of paper. When Louie walked out for lunch, everyone laughed. At the door he paused and turned around. "If you think someone is out to get you, it's paranoia. If someone is really out to get you, it's not paranoia." Fingers pointed and more giggles followed as Louie turned around again. A sign on his back said:

NATURAL DISASTER AREA

If you looked very closely, you could see the fine print at the bottom.

(By the way, it <u>was</u> Kara's pen)

2 Slugging It Out

*L*ouie came down the hall one morning, followed by a gang of kids. Something was brewing. Louie was early for a change. Someone in the group squealed, causing the whole crowd to draw back and laugh. Kids walking the opposite direction turned around to look, blocking the flow of traffic and creating collisions.

"Hey, look where you're going!" someone yelled.

Another voice called, "What's Tin Head up to now?" Sometimes the herd moved slowly and grew thick. Sometimes it moved quickly and thinned out. Mr. Calzone, the fourth grade teacher from across the hall, came out of his classroom to investigate. He loved excitement, especially in the morning.

"Hey, what's happenin'?" he boomed. He didn't have to push to get in front. (When you're as big as Calzone, it just happens.)

The object of everyone's interest was a fake banana slug that Louie had picked up at a joke shop. From a distance, it looked like a real slug. It dangled at the end of a long choke chain. When Louie jerked on the chain, the slug flew into the crowd of kids.

"What in the world is that?" Calzone barked.

"You don't know?" Louie said. "It's a banana slug. They're indigenous to this area. Surprised you haven't run into one."

"What are you doing with it?" asked Calzone.

"I'm trying to escort it to class, but it's hard to control in a crowd."

"It chased me," giggled a redheaded girl with freckles.

"Itth an attack thlug," squealed a small boy, with two front teeth missing.

"Sometimes banana slugs get excited," Louie said in the slug's defense. "They're very unpredictable when they get like that."

"Luckily it's dis-crim-i-na-ting though," smiled a small girl in large glasses.

"Oh, yeah?" said Calzone, raising his eyebrows.

"It only assaults girls for some reason," Louie explained. "I'm not sure why."

"Well, that's a relief!" Calzone exclaimed.

Ms. Kraut poked her head out of her door. "What's all the commotion out here?"

"Louie brought a slug to school," sang a little blonde girl, flashing her eyelashes and tossing her long braids.

"How revolting," scowled Ms. Kraut.

"How revolting!" scowled Ms. Kraut.

"It's a long banana slug with little antennae that stick out," squeaked a tall, skinny boy, holding his fingers above his head.

"Get that disgusting thing out of here!" squealed Ms. Kraut.

"It really likes girls," grinned Calzone, winking first at Ms. Kraut and then the kids.

The crowd laughed, but Ms. Kraut ordered, "Get to class, all of you. You'll be late." She shook her head. "Some people never grow up," she muttered in Calzone's direction, shutting the door with a bang.

Late as usual, Louie ambled into class carrying his slug. He set his duffel bag down gently to avoid breaking the liner of his thermos. Mrs. Butterhorn's warning was still fresh in his head from yesterday, "Louie, if you break that thermos liner one more time you're going to have to give up coffee."

As he tried to concentrate on his morning's work, Louie's mind kept returning to his pet slug. When Kara, who sat next to him, left to take a

message to the office, Louie got an idea. He
looked around to see if everyone was working.
Each head was bent over a writing project that
Mrs. Butterhorn had just assigned. Mrs.
Butterhorn sat at her desk correcting math papers.
It was a perfect time. With a little help, the slug
crawled out of Louie's desk and over onto Kara's.
It nestled comfortably on Kara's open spiral
notebook. Louie waited.

Pretty soon Kara came back. She was all
business in her red pant suit and matching
earrings. She read the instructions on the board as
she sat. Still reading, she picked up a brown and
yellow object and began to write. There was a
slight pause. As Louie watched, Kara's face
turned a pale gray. Her mouth opened wide.
Then she screamed, a loud agonizing scream, the
kind people scream if they see a ghost. All in one
motion, she dropped the slug, which she had
mistaken for a pencil, pushed her desk away, and
jumped out of her chair.

Mrs. Butterhorn appeared in a flash. "What in the world happened?" she asked.

At first Kara couldn't speak. She stared in shock at the contents of her desk that lay in a jumbled mess at her feet, her chair with its legs in the air. She looked up at Mrs. Butterhorn.

"There was a slug on my desk," she choked, wrinkling her nose, "I touched it."

A few giggles broke out across the room. "It's an attack slug," warned a boy, peering over thick glasses. "It goes for girls."

Louie tried to make himself invisible as he carefully pulled the choke chain on his slug. He had a few more inches to go when the chain caught on something.

He jerked lightly. Nothing happened. He yanked a little harder. Then he heard a voice above his head. "Louie, are you the owner of this slug?"

"Slug?" asked Louie. "What slug?"

"The one under my foot," Mrs. Butterhorn said with her teeth tightly clenched.

"What slug?"

Louie, tucked his head, hunched his shoulders and brought his elbows close to his body. He closed his lips tight, arched his eyebrows, and peered up at Mrs. Butterhorn. "Mrs. Butterhorn has never been a violent person," he thought. "But people are sometimes unpredictable. I'm no masochist," he thought, using a term he'd learned from his father, who worked in a psychiatric hospital. "I'm not fond of pain. I don't know how Mrs. Butterhorn will react to my little prank. I better not take any chances." He waited for Mrs. Butterhorn to speak.

Seeing Louie in such a vulnerable position, Mrs. Butterhorn took pity on him. "Put your slug away and help clean up this mess. Then, get back to work. There will be no more slug attacks in this classroom," she said with finality. Then she put her hand over her lips to catch a smile.

Louie got down on his hands and knees to help Kara. She said, "No thank you. I'll take care of this myself if you don't mind." Kara felt disappointed that Louie didn't get in trouble, but at least Mrs. Butterhorn spared her the lecture on overreacting. "When will Mrs. Butterhorn realize that living with Louie is impossible?" she fumed.

There were no more incidents in class that morning. Mrs. Butterhorn gave a science test about the properties of light. Louie came to a question about refraction. He took an old mirror out of his duffel bag. Imperfections in the firing process caused distortions in the glass. He liked to look in the mirror and make strange faces.

"Louie, put your mirror down and finish your test."

He read the next question about peripheral vision, staring in different directions to experience the effects.

"Louie, keep your eyes on your own paper," warned Mrs. Butterhorn.

"We will take the second part of the test after recess," announced Mrs. Butterhorn.

"Periscopes, kaleidoscopes . . . . It's all done with mirrors," Louie muttered to himself as he dug through his desk, looking for his slug.

Louie took the slug to recess and again gathered a crowd. "Meet Slime, the attack slug. Note the tentacles. His eyes are at the end. He's watching you. Look out! Though most slugs are plant eaters, Slime seems to have an unusual appetite for girls." He jerked the chain and enjoyed the screams.

The children saw Ms. Kraut, who had playground duty. "There's Sour-Kraut. Come on. Let's go scare the old fossil," tempted a large dark-haired boy. Ms. Kraut passed by, followed by her usual group of girls.

Louie led his group in the opposite direction. Kara Suko scowled at him. "Speaking of fossils," he lectured in an exaggerated voice. "Slime won't leave one when he dies. Think about it. He lacks vertebrae."

He heard Ms. Kraut say, "I hate slugs, especially long, slippery banana slugs." Ms.

Kraut hadn't gotten close enough to discover that Slime was a fake.

After recess, Mrs. Butterhorn's class went back to work on their tests.

"I don't see any questions on holograms. How am I supposed to show my understanding of laser photography?" Louie wondered aloud.

"No talking during the test," reminded Mrs. Butterhorn. Then she began to sniff. Soon everyone in the room was wrinkling up his nose and sniffing. The distinct smell of popcorn filled the air.

In the fourth grade class across the hall, Calzone was popping popcorn to reward his students for good behavior. As the students enjoyed their free time, Calzone thought about Louie and his slug. He thought about Mr. Gritz and the school rules. "I'm sure Gritz has a rule against bringing pets to school, especially dangerous pets." He picked up a large cylinder, opened a spout on the top, and poured some of the contents in his hand. He seasoned the popcorn, as he continued to think. "A school can't afford to have a pet assault . . . ." Suddenly his eyes bulged as if something was filling up the space in his head. "Salt!" he cried, snapping his finger. "That's it!" He closed the spout and said to his assistant, "Excuse me, I'll be right back."

Calzone quietly opened the door to Mrs. Butterhorn's room. "Good! Everyone's busy," he thought. Mrs. Butterhorn's head was bent over a pile of papers. She didn't notice him enter. The students' desks were randomly placed around the room, so it took him a while to find Louie. He finally spotted the back of his plaid shirt, completely on the other side of the room.

Calzone, wearing a blank expression, walked toward Louie. One hand, hidden behind his back, clasped a blue cylinder. He spied Louie's slug on the floor beside him, with the chain going up to his lap. Calzone tiptoed quietly, being careful not to disturb Louie.

One head turned and a single pair of eyes, framed in thick glasses, followed him across the room. When Calzone got close enough, he bent down. He opened the spout and poured salt over the slug. Only the chain and two eyes stuck out of a white dome.

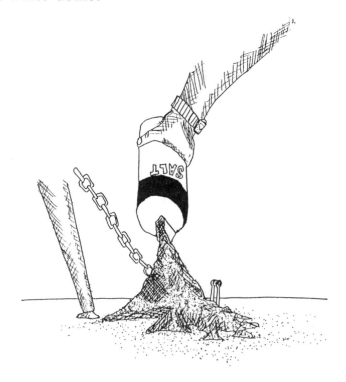

Only the chain and two eyes stuck out.

Then he got up, quietly turned, and made his way to the door. He had only three steps to go when he heard a muffled giggle, then one or two more. A ripple became a wave of laughter as more kids realized what he'd done. Louie finished his test. "I wonder what everyone is laughing about." He picked up his mirror to have a look. In the mirror, he saw a large, dark, deformed shape heading for the door. Out of the corner of his eye, he noticed his choke chain coming out of a curious white mound. He jumped out of his chair screaming, "Slime! Slime! What have you done to my pet slug?"

"I uh--salted him," smiled Mr. Calzone. "He had it coming."

"Slug assault! Slug assault!" Louie cried hysterically. "Poor little slug." Louie whined. "I'll save you, Slime." He knelt and brushed off the slug. Then with all the urgency of a paramedic, he picked the slug up and administered mouth-to-mouth resuscitation.

The kids all grabbed their stomachs, groaned, and recoiled as though they were connected parts of a single organism. Kara Suko leaned over to her neighbor and exclaimed in a voice that Mrs. Butterhorn would be sure to hear, "Now that's what I call overreacting." Mr. Calzone held his stomach with one hand and pointed a finger at Louie as he backed out of the classroom, shaking with laughter.

3 What's Cooking?

*L*ouie was a stare collector, a master at attracting strange looks. He could not possibly have gathered more gawks if he wore a sign that said:

Free Stares

(No limit)

He could fascinate a fleeing bank robber or hold a speeding motorcyclist spellbound. Louie could mesmerize a mother changing diapers on quintuplets.

How did he command so much attention? His wavy brown hair was a bit messy but hardly worth a second look. His brown eyes, though full of mischief, could not account for the sheer number of stares. Straight teeth hid innocently behind his lips, requiring neither braces nor dental headgear. His pants were last year's style, a bit too long, and lacked a belt, but they were not that interesting. These factors combined, could not account for Louie's record breaking success.

Louie's secret sat on top of his head. It attracted the attention of kids and grownups alike. Everyone took time out to stare at Louie's head, not just once or twice, but each time they saw him. People set aside their manners to gawk until either Louie disappeared or they bumped into something.

On top of Louie's head sat an authentic French World War I helmet. Louie bought it at an antique store. It was gray and rusty and full of dents. Louie wore it everywhere he went--to the library, to the post office, to the supermarket. Some people say he even wore it to bed. It was more than a trademark. "It's my life support system," Louie claimed.

Harmony Harbor Elementary School did not allow boys to wear hats indoors. The boys resisted the rule. They smuggled their hats into class, and wore them whenever they got a chance. Mrs. Butterhorn didn't care about the hat rule. Usually she didn't see the hats. She rarely even looked at the kids' heads. There were too many of them. She would say, at teachers' meetings, "I'm more concerned about what's going into their heads than what they're putting on top." The principal didn't agree.

Mr. Gritz declared, "No gentleman wears a hat indoors." He believed in etiquette and expected the teachers to enforce the "hats-off" rule. Mrs. Butterhorn tried, but most of the time she simply didn't see the hats.

If the boys wore their hats in the hall, Ms. Kraut would catch them. Then she would scold Mrs. Butterhorn. Mrs. Butterhorn got tired of being corrected by Ms. Kraut, so she made the "hat-check" rule.

"Boys," Mrs. Butterhorn would say as they entered the room. "Bring me your hats." The "hat-check" procedure became as routine as roll call and lunch count. Mrs. Butterhorn threw the hats onto a high shelf and only got them down at recess.

"A hat so rare as a French helmet should not be tossed up on the shelf like a common baseball cap," Louie reasoned. "I think you should capitulate," he smiled at his clever choice of words. Mrs. Butterhorn did give in but not because of Louie's logic. Enough falling baseball caps had hit her on the head to alert her to the potential risk of checking-in a battle helmet. She chose to ignore Louie's helmet. By sneaking through the halls, Louie managed to keep his hat on for weeks.

One morning, Louie had a little extra time before the bell rang, so he stopped off to see Calzone. Most of the students were in the room as Louie approached Calzone's desk. "Hey Metal Head, what's new?" a muffled voice rang from the back of the room. Louie chose to ignore the comment, and the chorus of giggles that followed.

He found Calzone at his desk organizing some paints. Every year Calzone's class built and launched model rockets. Louie liked to stop in and see how the project was going.

As Louie examined the rockets, the kids gawked at Louie and made comments among themselves. "He's screwy," said a large boy with freckles.

"Screwy Louie!" laughed a tall skinny boy. Calzone took a critical look at Louie's rusty helmet. It really was an interesting object. He secretly admired Louie for getting around the hat rule. Calzone believed rules were made to be broken. Schools were entirely too serious most of the time. He always wore a hat himself, and agreed with Louie that the hat rule, which only applied to the boys, promoted sexual discrimination. Of course he never let on to Louie about his true feelings. Instead, he made a game out of trying to get Louie to remove his hat. "Hey Louie, he said, I'll bet that rust is staining your hair. How would you like me to paint your helmet?"

"Would I have to take it off?" Louie asked wrinkling his forehead and raising one eyebrow.

"Only for a couple days," promised Calzone. "The paint dries fast."

"I don't know," Louie said. "I haven't had it off for a long time."

"Two days. That's all it'll take. Two days or a full refund," Calzone winked.

Louie tried to picture what his helmet would look like with a new paint job. "Refurbishing could increase its value. It might be a good investment," he thought. Silence fell over the room as Louie put his hands on his helmet.

"Note the detail work," he said to Calzone, running his fingers along the bumps, ridges, and dents. "Sometimes painting antiques hides the embellishments."

"Louie, when I get through, your helmet will be in mint condition," promised Calzone.

"In just two days?" Louie asked.

"Two working days."

Louie was taking a big risk. Could he trust Calzone? He took a moment to think. "One day Mr. Calzone hid Miss Strate's lesson plans. They were the ones she'd been using for five years. She got so upset, she had to take emergency leave. Mr. Gritz substituted. He played country music on his guitar and did Elvis impersonations. Once Mrs. Gumble asked Calzone to discipline a student, and she found Calzone and the student in the back of Calzone's room playing video games. When Mrs. Butterhorn got a new rolling chair to replace the one that tipped over backward with her in it, Calzone switched the chairs back."

"However, people can change," Louie thought, as he put both hands on the helmet.

"He's going to take it off," someone whispered. "Calzone is a practical joker," Louie thought, taking down his hands. "He usually only targets the teachers," he reasoned, raising his hands to the helmet. "That could change," he thought, removing his hands again. "So far, Calzone has not directed his twisted humor at a student," he debated, reaching for the helmet again. "Wait a minute. What about the assault on my pet slug?" He lowered his hands.

"The helmet helps him think," said a voice loud enough for Louie to hear.

Louie noticed the students. He rubbed the insignia on the helmet, adding thirty-three more stares to his collection. A French artist unveiling a new painting at the Louvre could not have commanded more attention.

The tardy bell rang. "You need to decide, Louie. You're late for class," Calzone boomed, standing taller and puffing out his barrel chest.

Louie began to twist his shoulders back and forth. He clenched his teeth. He drew in a deep breath and let it all out. "He's going to do it!" whispered a boy in the front row.

Silence fell over the room as Louie, with the exaggerated air of a French chef lifting the lid on a pan of steaming gourmet rabbit stew, removed his helmet.

Calzone studied Louie's hair. He scanned backed and forth, from front to back and from side to side. "Just doing a head rust check," he said smiling. Some kids ran up for a closer look. "Down in front," the others called.

Exhausted by the decision-making process, Louie headed to class. He didn't hurry, though he was now late. As he passed the outside row of children, he collected more stares and a trail of giggles. The weight of the helmet pressing on his thick hair had carved a perfect helmet ring. The helmet left a lasting impression on everyone, especially Louie.

Calzone gave the students some assignments for the morning and got right to work on Louie's helmet. He put it in the sink and began to rinse it. He scrubbed it with sponges and cleanser in the lukewarm tap water.

"This is worse than I thought," he said, stretching his eyebrows to their full height. "This calls for drastic action."

When his students left for computer class, Calzone put the helmet under his arm and strode down the hall. The helmet attracted several stares, but Calzone didn't notice. "I'm on a roll," he said as he passed a third grade class. "As they push lead to paper, history is in the making," Calzone announced, to anyone who might be listening. He passed a second grade classroom. Behind closed doors, students worked on their lessons. Yet, not one of them approached his task with more determination than Calzone. "I'm a man on a mission," he boomed, as he turned the corner toward the kitchen. Caught up in his own thinking, he failed to witness the collision of two gawkers and a television on wheels.

"I see this job as a four-step process," he spoke aloud in a serious tone. "Step one of the refurbishing plan calls for a run through the food service's commercial dishwasher. I'll pull out all the stops, push all the buttons, apply every chemical known to food processing," he laughed, enjoying his humor.

Calzone needed pot holders to carry the steaming helmet back to class. He held it out in front of him and warned everyone he passed. "Hot helmet. Don't touch!"

Like baby chicks in a row, a class of kindergartners followed their teacher as she led them to the library. "Shhh! Remember if you're quiet, we'll get another marble in the jar," she bribed.

Mr. Gritz walked by. He looked down the line and nodded approvingly. Lola Mae Hart was one of his favorites. "She has excellent classroom control," he thought to himself as he walked into his office.

At the sight of Calzone and the helmet, the kids' eyes widened and they fluttered around the teacher, pulling on her skirt and stepping on each other's toes. Three or four of the bravest followed

Calzone and the helmet down the hall, forming a small parade. The scene startled the children so much that, Mrs. Hart decided to take the whole brood on a detour to the restroom.

Unaware of the chaos he created, Calzone hurried back to his room.

"Hot helmet,. Don't touch!"

He scrubbed the helmet with scouring pads. When his students returned, they asked to help. They filled the sink with suds. They scrubbed and rinsed repeatedly. By the end of the morning everyone had finished their classroom work and scrubbed and rinsed the helmet at least once. "Now for the drying process," Calzone announced, as he placed the helmet on the heater and turned on portable fans. News of the helmet spread. At recess kids started dropping by to see the helmet. At first just the fifth graders popped in. Soon a few third graders showed up. Eventually someone from every grade had investigated the helmet, even kindergarten. After recess, Louie appeared, still wearing his helmet ring. Impressions last a long time.

"How are you feeling, Louie?" Calzone asked.

"For the first time in my life, I feel different," he said. "I've noticed people staring at me. When will the helmet be done?"

"We're right on schedule. It should be ready tomorrow afternoon," Calzone assured him. Louie shuffled his feet as he made his way back to class.

"Hey, Louie, how's it going?" a voice called. It was Chuck Roste, the tough kid on the playground. Louie's eyebrows arched in surprise. Chuck rarely spoke to him.

Just then Mr. Frankosky, the custodian arrived with the sandpaper that Calzone had ordered. "What took you so long, Frank?"

"Oh, it was the hotdogs for lunch. Some first grader got sick in the hall."

"Tough luck," called Chuck.

"Gross," cried a girl's voice, "Those hotdogs were green!"

"Camouflage dogs," blurted Louie. "I've been trying to warn everyone about the dangers of all-beef franks," he added as he returned to his classroom.

When Calzone handed out the afternoon's assignments, everyone got right to work. Before the day ended, all the kids had finished their assignments and sanded the helmet. They stood around admiring their work.

The next morning Calzone prepared for the final step, applying the paint. He chose semigloss black. "Too many dents for high gloss." The helmet soaked up three coats of Andy Cooper's Instant "No Mess, No Stress" Rocket Paint. Even with three coats the job wasn't perfect.

Calzone shook his head, "I should've primed that sucker." The only color he had for the trim work was light gray. He painted the decorative crest over the helmet from front to back. Then he stood back to admire his work. Putting his thumbs in his pockets, he rocked back on his heels. Suddenly the realization hit him. "The black helmet . . . the silver stripe across the top . . . . Oh, no! It looks just like a skunk."

Then Louie walked in to check on the helmet. After examining the shiny black dome, his eyes fell on the silver crest. Looking up into the face of Calzone, he asked, "Is this your attempt at humor?"

Calzone did something no one had ever seen him do before. He turned bright pink.

Louie's mouth stretched into a smile. "I like it," he said.

The helmet dried all afternoon and during the night. When Louie came to pick it up the next morning, it was ready for delivery. He tried it on. Something was different about it. It didn't feel the same on his head. It felt hard. He didn't mention any of this to Calzone. He walked down to the resource room.

That morning Mrs. Jensen, the reading specialist, couldn't hold Louie's attention on the National Geographic, although it was about Antarctica, his favorite topic. She pretended that she'd lost her glasses, trying to trick Louie into reading on his own. It didn't work. Mrs. Jensen thought about the progress Louie had made in his reading. In third grade, he said to her, "I think I could learn to read if I just knew the sounds." She had taught him the letter sounds, and now he read well. Today, however, Louie fidgeted and pulled at his helmet.

She sent him across the room to Ms. Kraut to work on his keyboarding. "You need a firm hand," Ms. Kraut said. "You need to conform to standards. A good dose of discipline is in order. Louie, tell me your goals. What do you want to be?"

Louie said, "I want to go to the South Pole to observe penguins in the wild."

"How do you plan to get there?" she demanded. Without waiting for an answer, she continued. "You'll need airfare. That costs money. You'll need supplies and equipment. You'll need to know how to write down your observations. If you expect others to believe your reports, you'll need a Ph.D. behind your name. So sit down and get busy. Keep your fingers curved over the keys. I don't think I need to tell you why."

Ms. Kraut had installed a row of straight-pins along the computer table, to keep Louie's fingers curved over the keys. The quilted pillow, used to raise him to the proper height, offered some comfort and a subtle hint that Ms. Kraut had his best interests at heart. "Type. Put your thoughts down," she demanded. Louie squealed as he dropped his wrists on the pin fence.

"I know! I know!" he blurted, lifting both hands high into the air, "Up, curved, and ready!"

Mrs. Gumble rescued him. "Time for speech." Louie struggled with his "R" sound. His hometown of "Surly" became "Sooley." His short "O" sound fared no better. "Surly Hall" sounded like "Sooley Hoal."

"My British accent keeps me from making the sounds that you so desperately want to hear," Louie explained.

Mrs. Gumble sat beside him, "You don't seem very cooperative today, Louie. What's the matter?"

"It's my helmet. It just doesn't feel comfortable like it used to."

Ms. Kraut called from the other side of the room. "You could remove it you know. It does violate the hat rule."

"I got an exemption," he said politely.

Mrs. Jensen came to his rescue. "Louie, we'll solve this while you're out with Mrs. Sanchez."

"She's teaching me to jump rope today," Louie remembered, as he left for the occupational therapy room.

Ms. Kraut just shook her head.

Mrs. Jensen said, "I've got an idea. Becky, do you have any felt in your art supplies?"
Becky Gumble rummaged through her cupboard and pulled out a large piece of olive-green felt.

"Sit down," said Mrs. Jensen. She draped the felt over Mrs. Gumble's head.

"What on earth are you doing?" fussed Mrs. Gumble.

Ignoring her, Mrs. Jensen grabbed some scissors. "I'll hold and you cut!" she called to Ms. Kraut. Using Mrs. Gumble's head as a model, Ms. Kraut cut a piece of felt in the shape of a bowl.

Just as she finished, Louie returned.

"Rope jumping's not going very well," he said, adjusting his helmet. "Also, Mrs. Sanchez wants to know if you've got any aspirin."

He noticed Mrs. Gumble. He looked her up and down. He looked at her shoes. He studied her suit and flowered blouse. He admired her hand-painted necklace and matching earrings. He stared at the olive-green bowl of felt on her head. Then he took a hard look into Mrs. Gumble's eyes. "You are always so well-put-together," he said in a most serious voice.

Mrs. Gumble smiled. "Why, thank-you, Louie." Ms. Kraut laughed right out loud.

But Mrs. Jensen, who always took Louie's

side in everything, said sternly, "Louie, remove that helmet, right this minute."

Louie removed his helmet for the second time in weeks. He lowered his head. His arms hung limply at his sides and his feet stuck together. Mrs. Jensen plunked the helmet on Mrs. Gumble's head. Mrs. Gumble squealed. Louie looked up in surprise. Mrs. Gumble hunched up her shoulders and made a terrible face. "What are you doing to me?" Mrs. Jensen handed her a mirror. Mrs. Gumble gazed at her reflection. Her hair was squashed under the refurbished helmet! "Get that old thing off my head!" squawked Mrs. Gumble.

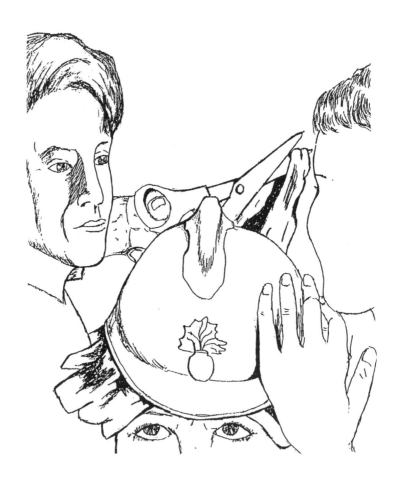

"Get that old thing off my head!"

"In a minute," said Mrs. Jensen, as Ms. Kraut made some minor adjustments with her large shears.

Mrs. Jensen removed the helmet. "What have you done to my new hairdo?" moaned Mrs. Gumble.

Ignoring Mrs. Gumble's wails, Ms. Kraut grabbed some glue and installed the felt into the helmet. Then she plopped the helmet back on Louie's head. He looked up, and smiled with his lips together.

Louie studied his special teachers--Mrs. Jensen, Ms. Kraut and Mrs. Gumble. A picture of Mrs. Butterhorn and Mrs. Sanchez popped into his head. An image of Calzone brought a smile to his lips.

Deep in thought, he walked toward the door. Turning around and leaning against the wall for one last look, he accidentally pressed a tiny button. The voice of the school secretary startled him. Miss Olive Pittman asked in her most businesslike voice, "How may I help you?"

Louie was too shocked to speak, but Ms. Kraut answered for him, "I'll have a hamburger, coke, and a large order of fries," For the first time in her life, Ms. Kraut had acted on an impulse. When the laughter died down, she added sweetly, "Oh yes, and could you make that 'To Go?'"

As he turned to leave, Louie declared, "There's a weirdo born every minute."

4 Getting a Bang Out of the Guy

The phone rang at Mrs. Butterhorn's house. She recognized the voice of Primula Twitwhistle, Louie's mom. "Say, we're having a little party, and we'd like you to join us."

"Oh?" said Mrs. Butterhorn. "What's the occasion?"

"We're celebrating Guy Fox Day."

"I'm sorry. I didn't hear what you said?"

"We're celebrating Guy Fox Day," Primula chirped a second time.

Mrs. Butterhorn frowned. She thought, "I have no idea what Louie's mother is talking about. I don't want to embarrass myself by asking again." Primula often brought up topics about which Mrs. Butterhorn knew nothing. These conversations made her feel foolish. "What may I bring?" Mrs. Butterhorn asked, hoping that food might provide a clue.

"Your family," said Primula brightly.

"No clue there," mumbled Mrs. Butterhorn.

"What did you say?" asked Primula.

"We'll be there," said Mrs. Butterhorn thinking fast.

"The party is November fifth, at 7:30 P.M." said Primula. "You may bring some snacks if you like. I'm glad you'll be joining us."

Mrs. Butterhorn thanked Primula and hung up the phone. As Mrs. Butterhorn prepared dinner, she tried to picture a "Guy Fox" party. She had heard of English fox hunts, and she had seen red fox in the area. "I hope Primula doesn't expect us to arrive on horseback." She smiled at the thought. "Perhaps I'll wear my red leather skirt and black boots."

That evening at dinner, Mrs. Butterhorn told her husband and two sons about the invitation.

"What do people do at a 'Guy Fox' party?" asked Eric.

"I have no idea," admitted Mrs. Butterhorn.

"Is it just for the guys, or are girls allowed?" Dane snickered.

"Only foxy ones," winked Eric.

Everyone looked at Mr. Butterhorn who was reading the newspaper at the table. He was a retired naval officer and worked as a deputy prosecutor for the county. He was precise, mentally disciplined and possessed strong powers of concentration. As he turned the page of his newspaper, he felt eyes on him. "Oh, oh, I'm in trouble for reading at the table again," he mumbled, folding the paper and setting it aside.

"William, do you happen to know anything about a Guy Fox?"

"How do you spell that?" he asked.

"I'm not sure," said Mrs. Butterhorn.

"The name rings a bell." His eyes rolled up almost out of sight. Knowledge filled William Butterhorn's head. It was just a matter of locating where he stored it. He often thought aloud. While he was talking, he usually stumbled on the answer. "I think . . . uh . . . yes . . . that's right. Guy Fawkes lived in England. He had some differences with the government, I believe. You know they have a parliamentary system in England. Are you familiar with how that works?"

The Butterhorn boys designed tricks to stop William Butterhorn's thinking process. Eric and Dane had a fear of being buried in piles of information, with only their arms sticking out. "Dad, your dinner's getting cold," Dane Butterhorn interrupted.

Mr. Butterhorn stopped talking. He drank his iced tea and ate his cold cuts in silence. Dane and Eric recognized the frown on his face. Mr. Butterhorn always got that look when he had to put his thoughts away before he was through thinking.

"After dinner I'll get out the encyclopedia," offered Mrs. Butterhorn, trying to smooth things over.

Mrs. Butterhorn had a little trouble finding Guy Fox, because she had the wrong spelling. She didn't want to risk asking William again, so she kept looking till she found the right topic. She discovered that Guy Fox was spelled "FAWKES." This famous Englishman lived in the 16th century. He and his followers tried to blow up King James I and the Parliament buildings, to protest religious persecution. The plot against the King failed, and Guy Fawkes met his death by hanging.

Eric rolled his eyes, "Sounds like a great excuse for a party."

The Butterhorns arrived at Louie's house. Eric and Dane raced to squeeze between the two Volvos, which were parked nose-to-nose in front of the walkway. Mr. and Mrs. Butterhorn walked around.

Dane opened the gate and the Butterhorns followed single file down the path. Eric knocked at the door. Louie greeted them. Holding a candle, he led them through the dark living room. A fire in the wood stove provided the only other light. "That's my room," Louie said, holding the flame so they could see the sign on the door to the left. Eric tilted his head sideways to read the words.

Louie's Room
NO ADMITTANCE

A screeching voice from behind the door startled them. "It's dangerous in there," Louie explained. "That's Loki, my magpie. Don't mess with him. He's vicious." Louie led them past a shelf on the right, where Mrs. Butterhorn set a plate of shrimp, cream cheese, and crackers.

Mr. Butterhorn looked around. He began storing things in his brain. He noticed an old presidential campaign poster, a program for a high school play, and a signed painting by

Chagall. A piece of fabric hung in the entrance to a room on his left. Ahead of him, a door led into yet another room. A 4.0 Honor Roll certificate with the name "Liz Twitwhistle" hung over the door. He recorded a Japanese lamp with no shade, an assortment of penguin cartoons, and a wooden ammunition box, overflowing with overdue public library books. From the kitchen a pot of chili threatened to boil over. Mr. Butterhorn's feet reported a change in texture, as he stepped off a Persian rug onto the bare kitchen floor. His brow wrinkled, as his brain attempted to classify and sort the images. Several house flies orbited his head.

Louie, tripping only once or twice, led them through the covered porch where a family of kittens nestled in a basket. They walked out onto the back porch. Mr. Butterhorn cataloged a discarded stove, a disconnected washer and dryer, and a used water heater. They climbed down the steps and into Louie's back yard.

Louie jumped about. "The Butterhorns are here!" he announced, leaping off the porch. He put the candle in a holder at the base of the stairs. After several unsuccessful attempts to get the candle to sit straight, he settled for a forty-five degree angle.

In the tilted candlelight, Mrs. Butterhorn discovered a blanket of fresh straw. She remembered Louie's Bantam hens and dozens of pigeons. "A layer of hay covers a multitude of sins," Primula whispered in her ear.

A small group of people sat around the bonfire visiting. Guests included the Twitwhistles' neighbors, and a few employees from the psychiatric hospital where Louie's father, Ralph, worked.

The encyclopedia evidently didn't tell the whole Guy Fawkes story. In a gory monologue, Louie painted an image of the hanging, quartering and burning of the notorious Guy Fawkes. Dane and Eric begged for more gruesome details. Mrs. Butterhorn's face turned pea-green.

Ralph explained, "Each Guy Fawkes' Day, English children dress up a dummy to represent the Guy. They go around town with a cup held out, calling, 'Penny for the Guy. Penny for the Guy.' They collect the money to buy fireworks for the celebration."

"Fireworks?" Dane's face lit up.

"Is it like our Fourth of July?" sparkled Eric.

"Better!" bragged Louie. "You'll see."

"Cool!" exclaimed Eric.

Mrs. Butterhorn squirmed. "Fireworks? Here?"

"I'll be right back," said Louie. He returned in seconds, pulling the Guy along behind him with a long rope. Made entirely of straw, the Guy looked almost real in Ralph's old polyester clothes. He had a noose around his neck. "We burn the Guy in the bonfire," explained Louie. "Come on, you can help me get him ready," he told the boys.

"We'll tie the Guy to our Pacific Yew tree. Our government is just starting to know the importance of these trees. I've known it for a long time. English craftsmen used the wood to make their bows. The bark contains Taxol, a cancer cure. Its branches are great for hanging."

The adults visited and ate snack food. Primula talked about her new job as a disk jockey on a local radio station.

Ralph introduced Dr. Harry Freudenberg, a psychiatrist that he worked with at the hospital. "We had a rough day today, eh Harry?"

"Oh, how's that?" inquired Mr. Butterhorn.

"We had seven Napoleons on the ward," Dr. Freudenberg groaned.

"And two of them were female," added Ralph.

Mr. Butterhorn interrupted the laughter, "That's easier to understand if you realize that there were actually three Napoleons. Napoleon the First was the most famous, a military genius." Dr. Freudenberg fidgeted as Mr. Butterhorn continued without taking a breath. "His son, Napoleon the Second, never became Emperor. The Senate called Louis XVIII to the throne instead." Dr. Freudenberg rubbed his beard. "The third Napoleon, Bonaparte's nephew, was a revolutionary. He tried to overthrow Louis Philippe, the King of France, in 1836." Dr. Freudenberg tapped his toe. "It was Louis Napoleon who wrote the 'Napoleonic Ideas' in 1839, idealizing the career of his uncle."

Dr. Harry Freudenberg displayed all the classic signs of someone about to be buried in a pile of information. "I think I'll add some wood to the fire," he blurted.

"Napoleon the First was not only a military genius. His ideas influenced French law."

Dr. Freudenberg piled several sticks on the fire. Mr. Butterhorn continued to prattle.

"He was short, about my height."

The doctor stacked some pieces of wood on the bonfire. Mr. Butterhorn's mouth kept moving.

"People nicknamed him 'The Little Corporal.'"

More logs went on, until the flames licked at the cedar and aspen trees.

"Pride and stubbornness led to his downfall."

"The Guy's ready!" Louie hollered. He cut the Guy down from the gnarled branch of the Yew tree, and drug him to the bonfire. He slung him up onto the fire. Within seconds, a large blast of firecrackers sounded. One rocket shot out of the fire, and then another!

"Where are they coming from?" squealed Mrs. Butterhorn.

"From the Guy!" Louie hollered over the noise of the explosions.

Mrs. Butterhorn was about to learn what "getting the Guy ready" really meant. Guy Fawkes had firecrackers in his head, Roman candles in his shirt sleeves, and bottle rockets in his pants. The crowd ducked as a bottle rocket shot sideways toward them.

Mrs. Butterhorn's knees shook. Her back stiffened. She thought of the straw beneath her feet, the cluttered porch, and the dry pigeon coop. She watched the flames lick the trees and the fireworks shoot out in every direction. The bottle rockets shot high over the trees toward the neighbors' houses. Pigeons flew in all directions and the Bantam hens squawked. Loki scolded everyone from his perch in the upstairs' window. George barked. The night sky over the lagoon danced with color.

She looked at Mr. Butterhorn, who was still talking. "Napoleon the First was defeated at Wa . . . ." He stopped in the middle of his sentence as a bottle rocket landed at his feet. His mouth froze in the shape of his last sound. His thoughts raced ahead, "Are these the 'Safe and Sane' fireworks we sell at the Harmony Harbor service club? Are they legal?" A siren screamed. Mr. Butterhorn's eyes shot out of sight, and his forehead scrolled, chasing his hairline.

Walter Twitwhistle scrambled up onto the chicken coop. "The neighbor's house is on fire," he cried.

With his features frozen in place, Mr. Butterhorn's mind raced ahead, "Oh, No! Will the police raid this party?" "I can see the headlines now, 'Deputy Prosecutor Caught Among Those Arrested At Illegal Fireworks Display. Entire Town Burns To The Ground.' Will this be the end of my career? Will this be my Wa . . . ."

Everyone but Mr. Butterhorn went into action. Ralph grabbed a bucket and started dousing the fire with water. The men and boys formed a bucket brigade around Mr. Butterhorn, passing buckets of water from the house to the bonfire. Dr. Harry saw that Mr. Butterhorn was frozen in shock: the whites of his eyes; the scrolled forehead; and the large puckered lips. Just then Louie came by with a full bucket of water. "What's wrong?" asked Louie.

"I think Mr. Butterhorn needs shock therapy," said Dr. Freudenberg.

"No problem," said Louie as he emptied the entire bucket of water on Mr. Butterhorn's head. "Waterloo?" sputtered Mr. Butterhorn, finishing his sentence, and spraying water all over Dr. Freudenberg.   Louie was nowhere to be seen.

"Waterloo?" sputtered Mr. Butterhorn.

"Let's move on down to the real bonfire," cried a party guest. Everyone raced down Surly Avenue.

Running toward the burning house, Louie looked up at Mrs. Butterhorn's terrified face. "Bet you've never been to a party like this before!" Mrs. Butterhorn gave Louie a blank stare. She shook her head back and forth in a hypnotic trance.

Surly's only fire engine, No. 811, barreled past. Flashing lights and screaming sirens announced the arrival of Engines 614, 615, 616 and a command vehicle from Harmony Harbor's District No 6. Three tanker trucks brought thousands of gallons of water. The sheriff, the fire chief, and the Medic Unit pulled up alongside the road. Louie dashed ahead to catch the action.

Mrs. Butterhorn took her time. Her mind whirled, "How could I, Catherine Marie Butterhorn, be caught in such a wild affair. I've taught hundreds of children never to play with matches. My Fire Prevention Posters hang at the state capital. There's more at stake tonight than a straw Guy in a polyester suit. My reputation may be going up in smoke." She waited several minutes before approaching the fire scene.

With her eyes on the ground, she picked her way through a maze of hoses and debris. She nearly stumbled into a fire fighter, who was barking out orders, "The fire's out. Let's break down and go home."

"That voice! I've heard it before!" Mrs. Butterhorn thought, looking up, past a pair of rubber boots, black pants, and a long yellow coat. She studied the blackened features of the fire fighter, partially hidden under a Captain's helmet. "Oh no!" she gasped. It was the face of the Great Rule-Maker, himself! She'd forgotten that Mr. Gritz was a volunteer for the Harmony Harbor Fire Department.

"Mrs. Butterhorn, what are you doing in this neighborhood?" Mr. Gritz barked in surprise.

It was the "Great Rule-Maker!"

Thoughts flew through her head. All color drained from her face. Then suddenly the blood began to flow back into her cheeks. Her eyes flickered, and a mischievous smile appeared on her face.

"Oh, I was attending a Guy Fawkes party," she crooned.

"What?" said Gritz.

"A Guy Fawkes party. Surely you've heard of him," she said with an exaggerated air.

Mr. Gritz was stumped. He looked at Mrs. Butterhorn in her red leather skirt and black boots. He thought, "I have no idea what she is talking about. I don't want to embarrass myself by asking again." Mrs. Butterhorn often brought up topics about which he knew nothing. These conversations made him feel foolish. "Wasn't he on the City Council?" Mr. Gritz asked, hoping for a clue.

"Well, he was involved in politics at one time," smiled Mrs. Butterhorn, touching her tongue to her cheek.

"No clue there," mumbled Mr. Gritz.

"What did you say?" asked Mrs. Butterhorn.

"I'll be right there!" called Mr. Gritz thinking fast.

"Shut down the tankers and the pumps on the engines. Disconnect the hoses. Let's go home! By the way, Mrs. Butterhorn, the guy who lived here should have listened to your advice. He could have learned something from your 'Just Say No‘ posters."

"What?" asked Mrs. Butterhorn.

"He smoked one cigarette too many."

"You mean a cigarette started this fire?" said Mrs. Butterhorn. Her eyes flared.

"That's right," Mr. Gritz drawled. "Nobody was home. Looks like a cat spilled an ashtray. That house contained stacks and stacks of old newspapers and magazines." As he turned to go, he added, "It made quite a bonfire."

Mrs. Butterhorn flinched at the word "bonfire." "So, it was a cigarette and not a bottle rocket," she whispered.

"What?" asked Mr. Gritz.

"So it was a cigarette and not a light socket," marveled Mrs. Butterhorn thinking fast.

Mrs. Butterhorn saw Louie walking toward her. He was holding a black and white cat. He appeared calm in the midst of the excitement. Mrs. Butterhorn always suspected that Louie was missing an essential ingredient. Now she knew. Louie lacked fear! Fright was not in his genes. She, Catherine Marie Butterhorn, had plenty to spare. She pledged to sprinkle a little fear on her Louie.

"I'll never forget this night," she promised herself. Mrs. Butterhorn had always gotten a kick out of Louie, but on Guy Fawkes Day, she really got a bang out of the Guy.

They returned to the Twitwhistle's, where Dr. Freudenberg stoked the fire and Louie prepared to finish off the Guy. "We must be going," said Mrs. Butterhorn, terrified at the thought of more firecrackers. Primula called, "Be sure to come back next year."

"Next year?" asked Mrs. Butterhorn, turning pale.

"Again? Next year?" Mr. Butterhorn squeaked.

Mrs. Butterhorn's body swayed. Her knees grew weak. At the thought of a repeat performance, Mr. Butterhorn's pupils disappeared.

He turned as white as a clean sheet, and keeled over backward in a dead faint.

"Shall I call the fire department?" asked Ralph.

"Not on your life!" exclaimed Catherine Butterhorn. A shot of adrenaline ran through her body. "Here, give me a hand with him." Dr. Freudenberg and Ralph Twitwhistle helped lift Mr. Butterhorn. They headed toward the car. Mrs. Butterhorn called,

"The party's been great!

Eric! Dane! Open that gate!

And as for next year . . ."

Interrupting, the Butterhorn boys waved their sparklers and chimed,

"WE'LL BE HERE!"

5 The Monster of Surly Lagoon

December arrived. Fog laced the crisp air--a fine day for Louie's eleventh birthday party. Louie, clad in army fatigues, and a battle helmet, took his place high in the hundred-year-old holly grove. He waited for his first guest.

Marsha Truffle arrived first. She was a big girl for her age, solid and sturdy. Her face was framed by blond hair, cropped short to reveal sparkling, sea-blue eyes. Mellow and laid-back, Marsha loved a good time.

"I feel like I've known Louie forever," she told her mother as they crossed Otter Bridge. "I discovered him at recess in third grade. My girl friends and I were following the playground assistant around. We were talking about dumb stuff. I was bored. Then I spotted Louie. He was wearing army clothes and a battle helmet. He was smoking a pretend pipe."

"When I asked him what his name was he barked, 'General MacArthur. Are you reporting for duty?'"

"Sure!" I said. "What do I do?"

"'I'm planning a major offensive at the southwest end of the playfield. It may be ugly. I could use a nurse.'"

" I told him I'd rather fight."

"And he said, 'I supported a woman in the last presidential election. I'm not sexist. You can be Captain Truffle. Just remember I'm a five star general. You take orders from me.'" Then he rocked back on his heels and took a puff from his imaginary pipe."

"He has an archaeological dig in his back yard. One day Rick was calling me names and teasing me about my weight. Louie stood up for me, 'Marsha's not fat. She just has big bones. Take it from an archaeologist.'"

"Here we are!" announced her mother. "Please be polite and have a good time at the party!" Marsha stepped out of a white sporty car. She wore a white jacket, white jeans, and a pair of sparkling white tennis shoes. A black and white package was held under her arm. It contained her present for Louie.

Two dirty-white 1964 Volvos, parked nose-to-nose, blocked the path to Louie's front door. "Seems like a strange place to park cars," Marsha thought aloud. One Volvo was missing a wheel. "Hope they weren't going anywhere," she grinned. She held the present in her left hand, ran her right hand along a hood and scooted sideways between the cars. "Made it!" she said, brushing her hand against her pants and leaving a black smudge.

Marsha paused in front of the gate to gaze at the scene ahead. She had forgotten the simple, primitive quality of Louie's home. In contrast to her modern house on Otter Island, the unkempt, bedraggled appearance of Louie's house sparked a surprising, yet pleasant sense of comfort and acceptance. Unlatching the gate, she eased herself through, trying to avoid the scraping sound of the rickety gate as it combed the pebbles. She locked the gate, crossing her fingers that it would hold. As her stiff new shoes pressed the spongy earth, mud gurgled and oozed around the rubber edges.

Suddenly, a loud banshee cry interrupted her thoughts. Louie, clad in army clothes and wearing his helmet, swept out of the bushes on a rope swing. She stepped back just in time, as he swung onto the path in front of her. Louie's traditional greeting should have come as no surprise. However, he was eleven, and getting a little old for such antics. "Louie, when are you going to learn to meet your guests in a civil manner?" Marsha asked with false sternness in her voice. Louie flashed his "no-teeth-showing" smile.

"You look as stiff as Styrofoam. My party will loosen you up."

Marsha laughed and turned to go into the house. She knew there was no point in waiting for Louie to join her. He would return to his hiding place to ambush the next guest. There would be no progress toward civilized behavior today.

She knocked on the door and waited for an answer. "What is it that I like so much about this house?" A horseshoe pendulum swayed above the door. "It's inviting," came the answering thought. A door chime made of local shells made a tinkling sound in the breeze. "It's unpretentious." Louie's magpie screeched. "So irregular." She studied a cobweb in the corner. "This house is 'user-friendly.'"

If the people in Marsha's world were unique, they didn't show it. Marsha felt unique and special. Louie gave her the courage to act out her feelings. The door opened. A black cat beside a blazing pot-bellied stove purred, echoing Liz's greeting, "Hello, nice of you to call."

The next to arrive was Rick Marconi. He and Louie met in kindergarten. Rick saved Louie from a fate worse than death. He agreed to be Louie's dance partner so he didn't have to dance with a girl. Rick admired Louie. He told his mother, "Louie needs help on simple stuff like spelling, reading, and math, but he understands big ideas. He helps at political rallies. Worrying about the spotted owl keeps him up nights. He even guards the ozone layer. But the part I like best about Louie is his imagination."

Rick wanted to get Louie something truly unique. He made his mom drive him over the bridge to an antique shop near the zoo, where Rick discovered a hand blown glass penguin, filled with colored glass. The clerk explained, "This craft originated in Italy, where creative artists found a use for the left-over glass after each work day."

A drip of glass below its right eye gave the penguin a sad look. "This penguin needs a friend like Louie," Rick thought. Looking the store clerk firmly in the eye, Rick frowned and spoke in a critical voice, "This penguin is pretty sad. You have to look at it closely to even tell it's a penguin. Few people would appreciate it. How about dropping the price?" He held out two whole weeks' allowance.

To his surprise the clerk said, "Sold." Rick smiled broadly, proud of his bargaining abilities.

At Louie's house, Rick bounced out of the car, waving a quick goodbye. He put his hands on the hoods of the Volvos and swung himself between the grills, landing on a pile of broken glass. Looking back, he noticed that the headlight ring was missing from one Volvo. "The landscape is always changing at Louie's," he mumbled.

Clutching Louie's present tightly under his left arm, he reached for the gate. The makeshift lock was still holding. He opened the gate. Its broken hinge screamed as if in protest of modern inventions. Rick smiled as he walked down the path.

He hadn't forgotten the traditional birthday greeting. Louie lived up to the meaning of his name, "famous warrior." Perhaps this year Rick could catch Louie off guard. In answer to his thoughts, a wild yell rang out of the bushes, "Banzai!" A deadly force propelled Rick to the ground. The birthday present escaped his grasp, and sailed high into the air. The launched missile landed in the prickly arms of the holly grove, the favorite roosting place of Louie's bantam hens. Thirty birds flew, squawking hysterically, as the brightly colored package sailed toward them.

Startled by the noise, George, Louie's mixed-breed dog, tore around the corner of the house. A male mallard duck, who considered George its mother, followed closely behind. George opened his mouth, ready to attack the would-be intruder. To the dog's surprise, a falling package hit him right between the jaws. He bit down hard. Stunned, George stared in wonder at Louie and Rick, who lay in a heap at his feet. Rick peered out from under Louie. "Good catch, George," Rick cheered. "Now give it up. That's a good boy."

"Logic always gets to George," Louie said, as he wrestled the dog to the ground. He yanked on the present to free it from George's clenched jaws. Louie stood up. He gave the gift a hard shake. "Obviously not breakable," he announced, handing Rick the package to examine.

Rick limped toward the door. George barked and jumped up on his legs. The mallard nibbled at his heels. "Down, George," Liz scolded, as she let Rick inside.

Another car drove up. Ali Abrams gave his twin brothers a quick kiss. "Yes, Lenny. I'll save you a birthday treat." Flashing a huge smile in his mom's direction, Ali called, "Don't hurry back!" He sauntered toward Louie's yard, inching his way between the two Volvos. Louie's father had performed another Volvo transplant since his last visit. As Louie would say, "The chrome bumper from the donor Volvo was successfully transplanted on the recipient Volvo." He picked at the bumper sticker that read, "I love my Volvo." Someone had added an "s." Now the sticker said, "I love my Volvos."

He looked back at the cars and down the street at the small town of Surly. "Louie has told me all about this town's hundred-year-old history. I can almost hear a stagecoach arriving." He took a deep breath. "I can smell the horses." For a moment he lost himself in time, listening to the faint rhythm of fiddle music.

He could hear Louie's lecture. "Surly began as a utopian community where people shared everything to have a perfect and peaceful life together. Sort of like Volvos sharing their body parts."

Ali giggled as the voice in his head continued, "They called themselves the Brotherhood."

Ali thought, "I'm not surprised that the Surly Commune didn't work. I have a hard time sharing with my three brothers. Most people aren't that good at sharing. It's different with Louie. He doesn't have much, but he shares everything he has--his ideas, his old junk, his time . . . . I'm lucky to have a friend like Louie."

Ali continued to think while balancing on the drain pipe. He opened the gate. With his eyes down, he investigated the ground with his boot. Chicken feathers flew as he kicked at a gunnysack, a hoe, a bicycle pump, and a Thermos stopper. "Keep your eyes on the ground, You never know what you'll find," said the voice in Ali's head.

A few steps from the doorway, Ali gazed up into the holly grove. Maybe this year Louie would spare him the traditional greeting. It was worth a try. "Hey, Louie, it's me, your friend Ali." The answer came in a loud primal cry, as Louie swung out of the tree, landing at Ali's feet. No one, not even his best friend, escaped Louie's ambush.

They laughed together and walked into the house, arm-in-arm. "Let the party begin!" Louie announced wearing his traditional smile.

Rick handed Louie the box containing the penguin. Rick was happy to give up the responsibility of protecting it from George, who considered it his property. "It's beautiful," exclaimed Louie tilting the penguin back and forth to catch the light. Rick explained the art of Italian glass blowing.

Louie tipped the penguin over, as if it was taking an exaggerated bow. He stopped with the bird upside down. "Left-over must have visited Japan," he said without emotion.

"What?" frowned Rick, leaning over to see what Louie was talking about. There it was, printed on the base in true penguin colors, "Made in Japan."

"Oh, no!" Rick whined, taking a deep breath and letting it all out. "I paid a fortune for a fake, left-over penguin? Let me have that. I'll take it back."

"Noooo!" cried Louie, with false hysteria. He jumped up and ran toward his bedroom, crying, "I'll save you, little left-over penguin. I'll save you!" Though he pushed against his door as hard as he could, it opened only part way. "Something's caught!" he squealed, pushing a little harder. The door opened another inch, allowing him to squeeze through. A sleeping bag threatened to block his way as he scrambled over a machete, tripped on an arrow, and mounted a camel saddle. He plunked the penguin on the low end of a tilted shelf, rearranging his oyster fungi, cobalt blue Bromo-Seltzer bottle, cracked crystal ball, and dead alligator, to make room for the new addition. "Everything in this room is perfectly balanced," he said. At that, Loki, his curious magpie, screeched and flew to the high end of the shelf. The board teetered dangerously, as Loki stretched and strained to study this strange new bird. Louie crossed his room now teaming with imaginary sharks, stepped on islands of dirty clothes, squeezed through a narrow opening, and closed the hatch.

He liked Marsha's book on Antarctica and a homemade card from Ali. Ali drew a group of emperor penguins dressed in their formal tuxedos. One penguin was wearing a World War I uniform. He was saying, "To celebrate your birthday, I decided to dress up."

Just then a knock at the door announced the arrival of Mrs. Rose Persimmons, Louie's favorite neighbor. She had stopped by with a very special gift that she had been saving all year. She presented Louie with a cigar box full of assorted treasures--keys that didn't go to anything, fabric scraps, old tokens, assorted bumper stickers, and a beautiful cobalt blue heart. As he studied the objects in the box, Louie's eyes danced and glazed over.

Ali waved a colorful box under his nose. "Earth to Louie! Earth to Louie! Remember me, Ali? You were about to open my present."

Ali helped him pull the ribbon off, and Louie opened a book of cartoons featuring his favorite penguin. "Birthdays are so stimulating!" he exclaimed, waddling around the room with his arms waving, his feet sticking straight out and his beak flapping.

The next package was from Liz. It contained three coins: a Kennedy half-dollar, a Buffalo Head nickel, and a Liberty dime. "I'll add these to my investment portfolio," he grinned. Then he stuck the coins into the cigar box. Walter brought out a strong rope to add to his network in the holly trees. Louie's parents gave him his last present. It was a newspaper from San Francisco dated Friday, October 20, 1944. The Headline in large, bold capital letters said, "MacArthur Rolls On!"

"People of the Philippines: I have returned," the newspaper quoted MacArthur.

Louie resisted the urge to read the whole paper. He smiled at his guests.

"What wonderful presents," he exclaimed. "Now I have something for all of you." He presented each guest with a small asparagus fern and two miniature ornaments, one red and one green. Everyone was grateful. The present came as no surprise. He gave them their first Christmas tree every year. It was a tradition.

Primula Twitwhistle announced from the kitchen that it was time for birthday cake. She entered carrying a chocolate cake with white frosting. A plastic penguin sat on an iceberg surrounded by a circle of licorice shark fins.

Ralph, started them out on the Happy Birthday song. Louie drew his head down between his shoulders and closed his eyes to make a secret wish. Liz cut the cake.

After the refreshments, Liz announced, "It's time for the games. The first game is Robot. The object is to take turns leading your partner around the backyard. Have fun! There's only one rule. Don't eat the poison berries."

Ali and Marsha were partners. Ali ordered Marsha left and right around the hazards in Louie's back yard. "Go right into the pigeon coop. Watch where you step! Go left across the abandoned row boat. By the way, have you had a tetanus shot lately? Go right through the holly grove. Better duck! The hens are roosting again! Eat the fruit of the deadly night shade," he commanded.

Marsha, the grand winner in the Merryview Hospital's "Poison Prevention Poster Contest" refused, "Yuck! This-robot-equipped-with-artificial-intelligence. I-value-my-life."

They passed Louie down toward the marsh. He kept spinning violently and shouting, "Short-circuit! Short-circuit!"

She heard Rick say, "Here comes Marshmallow. She'll save you!"

"Marsha, Quick! Rescue Louie with a kiss!" Ali ordered.

The answer came again in a high-pitched monotone, "This-robot-equipped-with-artificial-intelligence. I-value-my-life." Ali doubled over with laughter, forgetting for a moment his job at the control panel. Robot Marsha stepped on the head of a rake, that Louie had been using in his archaeological dig. A handle sprang up, hitting her on the nose and bruising her forehead. The game ended abruptly with Marsha complaining, "I'm seeing stars."

Next we'll play "Hide-and-Go-Seek-Murder," Ralph announced. "I've hidden clues to the murder. You are the detectives. You must find the clues and solve the murder. The grandfather clock holds the first clue." Everyone raced inside to read the message:

"A body you will find
Though not at Grandpa's knee.
It's lying in a tub with legs
Plum dead, as dead can be."

They found the dead body in an old bathtub under the plum tree. They recognized the victim as Walter, Louie's brother. He had a bread knife under his armpit. The kids discovered the rest of the clues around the yard. The kittens' bed on the covered porch held a clue. They found some information in an old clothes dryer. Notes were tucked under a broken Volvo clutch, between some records in a discarded phonograph player, and inside what the kids assumed was an abandoned beehive. It turned out that Louie was the murderer, and all the detectives and one angry bee chased him as he tried to escape from justice.

The last game was a treasure hunt for Spanish coins that Liz had buried about the yard. Like plundering pirates, the party guests took turns finding the coins with a map and a metal detector.

"I can't understand why Kara Suko passed up an invitation to this party," Marsha thought. "When I asked her if she was going, she said, 'You'll probably play pin the beak on the penguin, drop the clothes-pin in the helmet, or spin the antique bottle. I'll pass. I'm going to Pizza Games 'N Fun.' She doesn't know what she's missing. Nothing could compare to a party at Louie's place!"

Marsha hated to see the party end. She admired her Christmas tree and the tiny ornaments. As she fingered the red ornament dangling from the fern, it fell out of her hand and into the edge of Louie's archaeological dig. She reached for it. Louie came running. He hollered, "Red alert! Red alert!" Rick ran up behind him to see what all the excitement was about. Louie stopped short. Rick kept going. Louie fell into Ali. Ali bumped Marsha, who was already leaning over the pit. She lost her balance and tumbled into the muddy mire. "Oh no!" She cried, posing awkwardly on all fours. "Well, what the heck. Now that I'm here. I might as well find what I was after." She felt around in the slimy earth. She stretched as far as she could. Her slippery brown fingers touched something hard. Then it happened. She fell face down into Louie's pit. Seconds later she emerged with arms outstretched, covered in gooey mud. Clasping the prize in her fist, she peered through smelly, dark brown muck that covered her from head to toe.

Dark brown muck covered Marsha.

Ali gazed spellbound, not daring to speak. Rick, seeing the spectacle of Marsha covered in gooey mire, began laughing uncontrollably. Louie spoke, "At least she's biodegradable?" Rick shook with laughter. Holding his stomach with one hand and pointing with the other, he shouted between bursts of laughter, "Run. We'll be attacked by the lagoon monster."

Marsha wondered what her mother would say about her new clothes. She started to doubt her choice in rescuing the ornament. After all, she could have asked Louie for another one. "'Biodegradable.' That was a good one. Louie's right, I have lost that Styrofoam feeling."

Seeing Rick laughing and pointing triggered something deep inside Marsha. Rick was such a hard tease. Marsha had always been too unsure to take him on. However, just this morning her mom had mentioned the strong legs she had developed by riding her bike every day. An amazing burst of energy filled every fiber in Marsha's body. She sprang into action, leaping out of the pit and lunging at Rick. Caught off-guard by the change in mellow Marsha, Rick froze in shock.

Marsha came at him, belching out uncanny, monster-like sounds. As she reached for him, Rick let out a desperate scream and turned, running toward the front of the house. Down the path, past the front door, he sped. Knocking the hook loose, he slung the gate out of the way. Scrambling over the hood of a Volvo, he charged down Surly Avenue. The buildings became a blur as Rick raced for his life.

Marsha whipped through the open gate. All the party guests followed the brown trail of goo left by the angry monster. Marsha ran between the Volvos, balancing on a bumper and leaning on a hood.

The party guests, George, his duck, several pigeons, and Loki climbed on top of the Volvos for a better view. George barked excitedly and the mallard duck quacked. Rick ran past the Prescott's place, past Mrs. Austin's old house and garage, past Lucy and Frank's house, and beyond the hundred-year-old house.

At the end of town, Rick turned around and headed back down the other side of the street. Marsha stayed close on his tail. They ran past the Surly Post Office and the Town Hall. Louie led the spectators in cheers of "Look out! She's gaining on you! Watch out for the monster!" The pigeons squawked and Loki screeched, "Help! Help!"

At Granny Simpson's place, Rick showed signs of fatigue, and Marsha closed in. When Rick collapsed at the maple tree, Marsha Truffle went into action. She grabbed him, with her left arm around his neck, and her right arm under his armpit. The other party guests looked on in amazement as she picked him up, dragged him backward through the gate, and deposited him in the brambles.

Loki squawked "Ouch! Ouch!"

Marsha brushed her hands together. "That will teach you not to mess with the Monster of

Surly Lagoon.   Mother's right.   There is a reason for exercise.   I may be a marshmallow, but you got roasted."

Louie smiled in agreement.   "Never trifle with a Truffle."

6 Louie Finds a Snug Harbor

Mrs. Butterhorn required all her students to participate in a service project. She invited speakers from several service organizations to suggest ways the children could help in the local or world community.

Louie's favorite speaker presented the problem of preserving the rain forests. Louie had visited the local rain forests. He'd read about famous rain forests around the world. He cried when he thought about the extinction of animals who depended on these special environments. He raised his hand to speak. "Sensitive and bright animals, like the gorilla, live in the rain forests of Africa. They are not as fierce as they look. They are shy, friendly animals that need companionship and attention." He remained deep in thought. Meanwhile several girls signed up and turned the project into a bake sale.

"We can use the money to adopt a rain forest," announced a girl with wide blue eyes.

"I wonder how much money will actually get to the rain forest?" Louie grumbled.

"Yeah, Marsha would eat all the cupcakes," teased Rick.

Marsha gave Rick a menacing look. He shrank back into his place before Mrs. Butterhorn had a chance to correct him. "What do you mean Louie?" Mrs. Butterhorn asked, getting the conversation back on track.

"You have to go through so much governmental red tape."

"What is he talking about?" muttered one of the girls. "The school tape is beige."

Louie overheard them, and just shook his head. "A mind is a terrible thing to waste," he said seriously.

A speaker on Pro-Life legislation caught his attention. "We have enough people on this planet," he told the startled speaker. "People can be so greedy and selfish, especially politicians. Human beings litter, use aerosol sprays, and spill oil in the ocean. Actually, I prefer animals." The speaker frowned. He tried to cheer her up by showing her his "Celebrate Life" poster. He'd drawn a picture of two adult penguins and a pile of hatching eggs. The caption said, "Even penguins care for their young." She had to smile.

He was disappointed to learn that the "Easter Seal" camp program had no seals. "Our campers range in age from seven to ninety-nine," the speaker explained.

"People of all ages enjoy seals," Louie thought. "Seals are so cheerful and playful. They are almost as interesting as penguins." Before he knew it, that program filled up with rambunctious boys, who held visions of racing wheel chairs along camp trails.

He listened to the speaker on recycling. "We will provide three containers to sort your waste into glass, aluminum, and newspapers."

"What about brown glass, clear glass, green glass, magazines, tin, and plastic?" he asked.

The next speaker was from the school for the homeless. As the students discussed ways they could provide books and toys for these needy kids, Louie's mind wandered again. "Slugs are homeless too. No one appreciates them. They are homeless escargot. I could launch a campaign to 'Save the Homeless.' We'd have T-shirts with a slug on the logo." blurted Louie.

"Louie, this is a very serious subject," Mrs. Butterhorn reprimanded him.

"Some things are too serious not to laugh about," Louie defended himself. "I was fortunate to run across that statement last week," he whispered to Kara. The homeless were assigned to the care of Carlos and Mario.

"Save the Homeless."

He heard Mrs. Butterhorn's voice. "We have one more speaker left." She introduced Mrs. Clearview from Snug Harbor Nursing Home. The room got very quiet. "Rest homes smell funny," someone whispered.

"Sh!" warned Mrs. Butterhorn.

The director of the nursing home explained, "We need lots of help. Usually only family members visit the patients. Some families visit often. Others only come occasionally. At

Christmas time we have lots of company, but the rest of the year, the residents get lonely."

"Being different and feeling lonely go together," Louie thought. He thought about the caged gorillas that have died of loneliness. He put his head in his hands and closed his eyes.

"We also have other needs around the home," she said. "The lawn must be mowed and the flowers weeded. We have a little gift shop to manage. Someone has to prepare all the meals and feed the patients."

Kara didn't have a job yet. "I'll work in the gift shop."

"Rick and I can mow the lawn," offered Ali.

"I'll help feed the patients," Marsha blurted.

Rick started to say something, but he stopped himself. Louie opened his eyes. He raised his hand. "Who are the loneliest people in the nursing home?" he asked.

Mrs. Clearview thought for a moment. "Perhaps our Alzheimer's patients."

"Could you repeat that?" asked Louie.

"Some of our patients have Alzheimer's disease," she repeated.

"Old-timer's disease," blurted Kara. "It's when you get old and can't remember things."

Mrs. Clearview smiled, "Persons with Alzheimer's suffer from a disease that gradually destroys their memory. They forget who they are. They are lost inside themselves. Certain ones frighten people who visit, because they are unpredictable and do not act normally. They might get caught on a thought and repeat the phrase over and over. Sometimes they get angry and aggressive. It is hard for families to visit, because the patients do not always remember them. This makes the families of the patients very sad." The room fell silent.

Louie cleared his throat. "I would like to work with the Alzheimer's patients."

The next day Louie went to visit at Snug Harbor Nursing Home. Mrs. Clearview led Louie into the recreation room where the persons with

Alzheimer's met for their afternoon activities.
Though Louie wore his helmet, no one stared.
She introduced him to the nurse and her assistant.
He met over twenty patients. Soon Louie began
to get the names mixed up. "I have
'Sometimer's Disease,'" he muttered.
"Sometimes I can remember, and sometimes I
can't." Miss Jones smiled. She showed him the
patients' biography books. The books contained
photographs and descriptions of the residents'
lives. "This helps a lot." He read about Mr.
Edwards:

> L. Edwards was drafted into the army
> when he was only seventeen years
> old. The army had trouble finding
> shoes for his very big feet. When his
> troop went marching, they left him
> behind. His captain sent him on an
> errand to deliver a message to Major
> Douglas MacArthur. That is how he
> accidentally met one of our country's

most famous soldiers and became a runner for the army. His big feet probably saved his life.

"Wow!" exclaimed Louie. "I'd like to meet Mr. Edwards."

"Mr. Edwards and some other patients have gone on a field trip in the LOVE VAN," Mrs. Jones explained.

Several patients sat around a big table. Janice Jorgens placed clothes-pins in a can and removed them. Angie Haines folded and unfolded a dress pattern. Betsy Freeborn removed the binding from old calendars and Lucy Goodwin trimmed the edges with scissors.

Francis Spencer, a former school teacher, talked. Her sentences were complete and grammatically correct. She said all her sounds clearly. She laughed aloud and used lots of expression, but her words made no sense. The nurse said she was making "word salad."

Esther Samuelson sighed, "I'm so sleepy. I just want to go to bed." Betty Willis kept saying, "Wet floor," though the floor was perfectly dry.

Alex Malone sneezed, not once but seven times. He rubbed his nose until his face turned red.

Louie noticed a man in a tall ten-gallon hat. Louie whispered to the nurse, "Our principal thinks gentlemen should not wear hats indoors." Albert Hathaway slowly removed his hat.

George Frees lay on the floor surrounded by clocks. He played with an alarm clock and talked to himself. "Time flies," thought Louie.

Ann Benton walked rapidly around the room. She grabbed Louie and pulled him along with her. Her strength surprised him. He felt uneasy. She began to run, towing Louie with her.

Mrs. Jones said, "Ann, be gentle." Louie dug in his heels to stop. He reached out his right hand. Ann let go of Louie's arm long enough to shake his hand. "It worked! I'm free!" Louie thought.

"Thanks for the walk," he said firmly. "Let go now." Ann let go of his hand and took a seat in the corner of the room. She folded her arms and lowered her chin.

Mrs. Jones suggested, "Betty likes to read signs. Why don't you find her a new sign to read?"

Louie walked Betty around until she spotted a sign. She read, "Please, empty your own ashtray." She read it over and over.

Louie sat by Esther Samuelson. She complained, "I'm so sleepy. I want to go to bed." He tried a special technique that Mrs. Jensen taught him, "You're sleepy and you want to go to bed."

"Oh, yes," her eyes lit up. "Honey, I'm so sleepy and I want to go to bed."

Louie thought fast, "What do you think this is, a rest home? There's plenty of work to do around here." He helped to tear the bindings off last year's calendars.

Louie noticed Tom Gills. He sat in silence for a long time. His faced was frozen in anger. Only his eyes moved to avoid Louie's gaze.

He watched Judge Lane try to free his wheel chair. His eyes followed Ann Benton who began again to run around the room. He looked at the quiet patients who had not had any attention yet.

Esther Samuelson had begun to clean off the counter. He heard the nurse say, "Why Esther, it's wonderful to see you up and helping."

"Please empty your own ashtray," said a cheerful voice. No one was smoking. The nurse taught Betty a song to get her mind off the sign.

The session ended with a game of beach ball around a big table. The nurse's helper passed out visors and hats for the team to wear. George got a pointed hat with a feather. Ann snatched a straw gardening hat. The nurse decorated heads with baseball caps and colorful visors. Esther looked unique in a Styrofoam pith helmet, with a bite out of it. Albert Hathaway wore his cowboy hat.

Louie adjusted his French World War I helmet. "I feel right at home," he announced.

The nurse threw a large beach ball into the center of the table. The players batted the colorful ball back and forth.

Jo Bernam complained, "I'm no good at this. I might as well get my own team."

"You're great," Louie encouraged her. "Go ahead. Hit it!" Jo gave the ball a hard whack.

Esther started to speak "I'm so sleepy . . . ." Just then the brightly colored ball came her way. She returned it with a powerful smack.

Two hours passed quickly. The orderlies arrived to take the patients back to their rooms. Louie touched each resident. He waved goodbye. Jo smiled. Edward glanced away. Betty sang her new song,

"You are my sunshine, my only sunshine.
You make me happy when skies are gray.
You'll never know dear, how much I love you.
So, please empty your own ashtray."

Louie needed to talk. He was full of questions. "What causes Alzheimer's disease? Is it catching? Is there a cure? Why is Tom angry? Why don't you just let Esther sleep? Can you die from this disease? Aren't all old people forgetful?"

The director tried to explain. "Some of your questions have no answers. There is no cure for Alzheimer's disease. The disease may be hereditary. The patient's brain gets tangled. It can happen to any of us. It's hard to grow old. Persons with Alzheimer's need constant care. Care is expensive. The job is demanding. We do have laws that protect these special people. Some people expect everyone to fit in. Their ideas frighten me. The world is moving too fast. These people are left out. Old people don't want to be a burden on others. Yet, many of them need help." Fear spilled out of Mrs. Clearview's tired eyes.

Louie eyes watered too. "Some people believe in euthanasia," Louie said. "I'm not sure

how I feel. Killing is serious. It can't be cured.
I'd like to help."

"You could become an ethicist," suggested
Mrs. Clearview.

"What's that?" asked Louie who was always
fascinated with new words.

"An ethicist helps people make fair laws."

"You mean someone who keeps the
politicians in line," said Louie.

"You might say that," smiled Mrs.
Clearview.

"I've always planned to be a naturalist. I
wanted to study penguins in the wild, but
Antarctica is looking pretty bleak."

"Maybe you could do some research on
Alzheimer's, and develop a treatment."

"I've been thinking. Curing Alzheimer's
disease might be like repairing old Volvos. The
problem is small. Someone just needs to take the
time to find the solution. I could become a
molecular biologist. But that will take years.
These people can't wait for me to grow up.

They need help right away. You need more
hands. I'll recruit some kids. I'll advertise."
As he left, he announced in his MacArthur
voice, "I shall return."

The next day in school, Louie made a sign:

Wanted:	**Volunteers for Snug Harbor Nursing Home**
Job:	**Working with persons with Alzheimer's**
Qualifications:	**Must care about special people**

Alzheimer's patients are neat.
They're unique.
And they wear hats!

Louie Twitwhistle Ph.D. (Phony Doctor)

7 Left-Over Louie

*P*rimula Twitwhistle woke Louie up for the second time. "Get up or I'm sending in Loki."

"O.K." groaned Louie. He still had scars on the back of his neck from the last time Loki forced him out of bed. Primula went into Louie's room to give him his "cuppa." Louie sat up in his sleeping bag and drank his coffee and cream. He crawled out of bed and put on the clean clothes that Primula had laid out for him. Then he went into the bathroom to wash, comb his hair and brush his teeth. He heard his mom calling from the kitchen, "Louie, you're going to miss the bus." Primula put a fresh thermos of coffee in Louie's duffel bag. She put in a brown paper bag that contained a powdered sugar donut and a peanut butter and jelly sandwich. Louie never ate the peanut butter and jelly sandwich, but Primula always packed it anyway. "Louie, I wish you'd eat a more balanced lunch. I worry about what Mrs. Butterhorn will think."

"School is no place for eating," Louie explained.

Primula, George and his mallard walked with Louie to the bus stop, which was about a block away. "I don't see why the bus driver can't stop at our house. It would give me five more minutes to sleep in," Louie mumbled with his mouth opening into a yawn.

Louie was not a morning person. On weekends he stayed up till dawn watching old science fiction movies. It usually took him until the next Saturday to get his body back on day shift. It was only Friday.

Mrs. Butterhorn arrived at school a little earlier than usual. She had never planned a practical joke before and wasn't sure where to start. Ever since the Guy Fawkes celebration, she'd been thinking of a way to instill a little old fashioned fear in Louie. After all, fear was a survival skill, and should be included in a complete educational package.

Calzone stopped her in the hall. "Hey, would you like to order lunch off my 'Road Kill and Grill Menu?' Today's specialty is Porcupine Patties. 'We split 'em. You spit 'em.' Or how about Rancid Raccoon Skewers Served Over Rice? 'We poke, You choke.'"

Mrs. Butterhorn was in no mood for Calzone's humor. "I brought my lunch today," she waved. "Thanks anyway." She opened the door to her room and went inside. She corrected some papers and wrote some lesson plans, but her mind was on Louie.

By 9:00 A.M. the kids had all arrived, even Louie. Mrs. Butterhorn still hadn't thought of a plan. Still thinking, she called roll and collected the hats. "Kara, please pass out the lunch menus for next week," she said.

Kara laid one on Louie's desk. He handed it back. "I never eat hot lunch," she heard Louie say. "I'm a vegetarian. Remember last year? There was a boy in our class named Billy Burger. The teacher said he moved away. But I know what really happened. The food service got him. They served Barbecue Billy Burgers on field day. I don't like the idea of ending someone's life for a meal, when you could get by with a simple salad." Kara ignored him and continued to pass out the menus. She'd heard his stories so often.

At lunch time Louie got out his brown bag lunch. He noticed the hot lunch kids coming back with their trays. Louie looked at the meat loaf. "Hope you enjoy your corpse," he said to Julienne Beane who sat on his left. Juli always ate hot lunch and she couldn't afford to miss a meal. "Her arms are so thin, she can fit them through the three rings of her notebook," Rick teased. She didn't touch her meat loaf or reddish-brown gravy. Louie opened his thermos and poured himself a cup of coffee. He dunked his donut and began to eat.

"Hey Louie. Stop slurpin'," called Sam Sakamoto.

Louie shook his head so that his hair flew back and forth.

"Gee, Louie. Mind your manners," Sam called. "You're acting like an old crab."

Rick laughed and slapped his hands on his knees. "Crab Louie!"

Louie shook his head harder. "There are no crustaceans in our family tree." His hair flew further and faster.

Juli opened her mouth to take a bite of her cookie. Louie's hair flew right in her mouth. "Ahhhhhhhhhh!" Juli yelled, running to the sink to spit out cookie crumbs and hair.

Suddenly an idea popped into Mrs. Butterhorn's head.

While the kids finished their lunches, she rummaged around at her desk. She uncovered a copy of the school lunch menu. A Calzone smile appeared on her face. She sat at the computer and began to type. In a few minutes she looked up. Now was the time. Louie was out of his seat. She took the paper that she'd typed and placed it on Louie's desk. Louie returned and discovered what appeared to be a Harmony Harbor School lunch menu.

"Hey, what's this lunch menu doing here? I told you, I never buy hot lunch."

"I think you'd better read it to the class," said Mrs. Butterhorn.

Louie read aloud the Harmony Harbor School Lunch Menu. "'Presenting our Vegetarian Alternative.' Well, It's about time!" he exclaimed. He continued to read, "'Monday--Crab Louie.' Hey! Vegetarians don't eat crab."

"Keep reading," urged Mrs. Butterhorn.

"'Tuesday--Louiesagna.' Wait a minute. What is this?" said Louie, raising his eyebrows. "Wednesday--Louie Burgers, Thursday--Louie Loaf," he read, starting to get the picture.

"Friday--Left-over Louie!" he wailed, rising up out of his chair. A loud roar filled the room. Louie waved his arms and legs in false hysteria. He shook his head violently, until his helmet fell off. Just then the recess bell rang.

Everyone ran over to Louie's desk to see the menu.

"The fun is over. Everyone go to recess," said Mrs. Butterhorn.

The kids filed out of the room. "Come on, Left-over Louie, I'll save you," said Rick laughing aloud.

In the confusion Louie forgot to put on his helmet. Still discussing the vegetarian menu, Louie and Rick walked over to the baseball diamond to talk to Ali, who was waiting for a turn at bat.

Louie reached up to scratch his head. He realized his head was bare. "I need to go back for my helmet. It's my life support system," he said to Rick. At that moment a long wooden object flew through the air, hitting Louie in the back of the head. He fell to the ground, knocked-out cold by a flying baseball bat.

Everyone came rushing over. Ms. Kraut had playground duty. She moved in circles wringing her hands and crying. Ali ran into the school to tell the office. Mrs. Butterhorn, Mrs. Hart, Mr. Frankosky, and Mrs. Jensen came running onto the field. Everyone was worried about Louie. They tried to keep the kids on the playground back, so Louie could breathe. Someone called the ambulance. Louie heard the voice of Chuck Roste in his ear. "I'm sorry Louie. It was an accident."

Louie felt himself floating into the air. As he looked down, he saw two men wearing white coats coming toward him. They knelt beside a familiar form lying a few feet from home plate. The taller one grinned at the unconscious form on the ground, "Your time has come, Louie." They put him on a wheeled stretcher and rolled him across the field. Louie floated after them feeling strangely uneasy. When the attendants reached the parking lot, they headed for a white van. They loaded the limp form on the stretcher into the van.

Louie, floating high above them, looked down at the sign on the van. He cried out, "Help! Help! There's been a terrible misunderstanding." But no one seemed to hear him.

As the kids waved goodbye to the Harbor Ambulance, Louie, saw something that nobody else saw. For him the sign on the van read, "FOOD SERVICE," and a green sticker on the bumper announced,

"COMING SOON TO THE CAFETERIA NEAREST YOU--OUR VEGETARIAN ALTERNATIVE."

Left-over Louie.

8 Long Live Louie

*T*he weekend seemed endless to Kara Suko. Restless and impatient, she couldn't keep her mind on anything. She couldn't concentrate long enough to practice the piano or clean her room. The clothes she chose to wear didn't match. She misplaced her best earrings and left her homework half finished. Monday came as a relief. It was time to go back to school. Her mom gave her a ride so she could be the first to arrive. Kara couldn't understand the strange feelings that Louie's accident had stirred in her. She wanted to know how things had gone at the hospital. She couldn't admit this even to herself, but she was worried....worried about Louie Twitwhistle.

Kara arrived before any of the busses. When she entered the classroom, Mrs. Butterhorn was bending over some work at her desk. Kara thought about asking her if she'd heard about Louie, but some unknown force kept the words inside her mouth. Every few minutes, the door opened and another group of students walked into the classroom. Kara looked up to see if Louie was among them. "No sign of him," she thought.

Normally the students were boisterous and talkative as they entered the room. This morning an eerie silence fell over everyone who entered. Even Rick and Ali who often started the day with a playful race across the room, went straight to their seats. Sam Sakamoto did not jump to check his height on the door frame. His feet never left the floor. It was as if a sign hung in the doorway. "Remember Friday!"

The bell rang. Everyone took their seat. Everyone, but Louie. "Please stand for the flag salute," said Mrs. Butterhorn in a clear, flat voice.

"I pledge allegiance . . . ." the class began automatically and in unison.

"Take your seats for roll call," Mrs. Butterhorn continued.

"Is it my imagination, or is her voice softer, duller than usual?" Kara wondered.

The roll call began, "Ashley Applegate?"

"Here," came the response.

"Julienne Beane?"

"Here."

"Cheryl Chapman?"

"Here."

"D.J. Dodsworth?"

"Here!" said D.J. who normally answered, "Yo!"

"Sam Sakamoto?"

"Here!" said Sam who always had to be called on twice.

Kara's mind wandered and Mrs. Butterhorn's voice faded into the background.

"Kara Suko?"

"Here," stuttered Kara breaking the perfect rhythm of roll call.

"Marsha Truffle?"

"Here."

"Louie Twitwhistle?"

Silence fell as the beat of roll call stopped. Now was the time. Mrs. Butterhorn would speak the awful truth. She would pronounce Louie Twitwhistle . . . dead.

"Louie will not be with us today," Mrs. Butterhorn began in a halting voice.

"Here it comes," thought Kara, covering her face. She looked through her fingers at Ali and Rick. Their complexions were ghost-white. She looked into the faces of her other classmates. Large tears welled in Marsha's eyes. No one spoke. She looked back at Mrs. Butterhorn.

Mrs. Butterhorn fought back tears. She blew her nose and tortured herself with thoughts. "It was my little practical joke that started all of this. It was my fault that Louie wasn't wearing his helmet. If I had minded my own business, left well enough alone, been more professional-- none of this would have happened. It was all my fault." To the children she said, "Louie will not be with us today, or tomorrow, or even next week . . . " her voice drifted off. She wiped her eyes with a tissue.

Just at that moment--just as Mrs. Butterhorn was about to break the news, an alarm sounded. Like a jolt of electricity, the screaming alarm sent Mrs. Butterhorn into action. "It's the earthquake alarm. You know what to do, everyone." The students dove under their desks. Mrs. Butterhorn ran for cover.

When everyone was safely under their desks and the noise died down, Mrs. Butterhorn started an activity designed to keep their minds off the disaster. She called out, "What's four times five?"

"Twenty" came a high-pitched weak voice.

"I can't hear you," Mrs. Butterhorn sang over the rustling furniture.

"Twenty," came an answering chorus.

"Six times five?" Mrs. Butterhorn commanded.

"Thirty," rang a clear unison voice.

Mrs. Butterhorn gave the pitch for the school song. They began.

"We are discovering how to grow
In a harmonious way, you know.
Our great school is the one,
Where we all are winners,
And we all have fun . . . ."

Just then the classroom door opened.

Peering out from under her desk, Mrs. Butterhorn could only make out the feet and legs of the person at the door.

Only the feet and legs were visible.

Though the visitor did not speak, there was no mistaking his identity. Only one person at Harmony Harbor Elementary School wore cowboy boots. It was Mr. Gritz.

Mrs. Butterhorn felt a rush of pride. She had executed the earthquake drill perfectly. Every student crouched under a desk. The class was under perfect control. Mr. Gritz could not have popped in at a better moment. This would look good on her evaluation. "Why," she wondered, "I doubt if Ms. Kraut herself could have pulled off such a perfect drill."

"Mrs. Butterhorn," rumbled Mr. Gritz. "Might I asked you what you are doing?"

"The children have been reciting the multiplication tables, sir," Mrs. Butterhorn called from her hiding place. "We were just starting to sing our school song. We are doing just as you instructed us to do in the event of an earthquake."

"That is quite commendable," drawled Mr. Gritz. "Except for one minor problem . . . ."

"Oh, what's that?" asked Mrs. Butterhorn innocently, as she crawled out from under her desk.

"I am trying to conduct a fire drill!" thundered the voice of Captain Gritz.

Mrs. Butterhorn lost all the color in her face. She did not speak. She meekly followed the crowd of squealing students as they charged past Mr. Gritz, who stepped out of the doorway, just in time to avoid being trampled.

Once outside, the students took over. They ran to their appointed station on the field. Every other class was already assembled. The students chattered wildly among themselves. Mrs. Butterhorn didn't even try to quiet them although Mr. Gritz had a "No-talking" rule at fire drills. She saw Ms. Strate standing with a line of students. She heard Mr. Gritz say, "We would have made a new school record if Mrs. Butterhorn's class had been at their proper station, OUTSIDE." Mrs. Butterhorn looked the other way.

Soon the alarm rang to return to the school. The students talked among themselves and with students from other classes. Everyone was curious about why they were late. Small groups of students whispered and giggled among themselves.

By the time they got back to the room, the earthquake story had been told many times. The laughter died down and the students returned to their seats. Slowly, everyone began to remember what they had been discussing when the alarm sounded. They had been talking about Louie. A new hush settled on the room.

"Please take out your pattern blocks," said Mrs. Butterhorn in a tired voice.

"But, Mrs. Butterhorn," called Kara. "You didn't finish the roll call."

"Oh, yes. Now where was I?" she finished reading through the list without waiting for responses. She had seen them all at the fire drill. "Valerie Velez, Wally Wang, and Zelda Zagorski."

"Kara, please take the attendance form to the office," she said in her most business-like tone.

"But, Mrs. Butterhorn . . ." Kara started.

"No buts, young lady. We've wasted enough time this morning."

Kara got up from her desk. Picking up the attendance form, she made her way out the door. "I can't believe that Mrs. Butterhorn has forgotten about Louie so soon. I can't believe that Louie is dead," she thought. "Yet, there it is in black and white. Louie's name is deleted from the attendance form. Mrs. Butterhorn has made a straight line through his name for the rest of the month! Louie is gone forever. I can't understand how Mrs. Butterhorn can be so unfeeling," Kara's troubled thoughts continued.

On the way back from the office, Kara almost bumped into Mr. Calzone who was heading down the hall. "Hey, what's happenin'?" he boomed.

Getting no response, he looked down into Kara's dark eyes. "Hey, why the long face?" he asked. "If you're not careful, you'll step on it."

Calzone's worn out joke didn't work. Kara's expression did not change. Tears filled her eyes. "Louie Twitwhistle is dead!" she blurted. "There! Now I've said it." The awful words were out. The horrible truth had been spoken.

Calzone stopped. "What?" he asked in disbelief. "How do you know?"

"I just know," Kara wailed.

Calzone put his arm around Kara. "Come on. I'll walk you back to class," he said softly. He escorted her to her seat. He paused to study the empty desk beside her. The contents threatened to break out. At the foot of the desk sat a faded blue duffle bag, with a telltale trail of brown coming out the side. These were the only signs remaining of Louie. Slowly Calzone made his way to Mrs. Butterhorn's desk. As she sat, correcting papers, a large shadow fell over her desk. She looked up in surprise. "Catherine," Calzone whispered, "Is it true?"

"Is what true?" Mrs. Butterhorn asked.

"About Louie Twitwhistle?" Calzone asked, raising his eyebrows to show concern. "Is he really dead?"

"Dead?" Mrs. Butterhorn exclaimed. "Good gracious, no! I just talked to Primula Twitwhistle this morning. He's in the hospital, but he's very much alive."

A chorus of cheers spread across the room. Kara's face shone. Then it wasn't true. Louie was alive!

Rick and Ali jumped up and did a little celebration chase across the room. Marsha Truffle started a chant. "Louie lives! Long-Live-Louie. Long-Live-Louie." Sam Sakamoto leaped high into the air.

Kara sat back in her chair and sighed a big sigh of relief.

"Before you get too excited, you need to know that Louie has been in critical care. He had a very bad head injury and he won't be back to school for the rest of the month. You may make cards for him in your spare time. I will be delivering them on Friday when he's feeling a little better."

"You can't keep a good guy down!" Calzone cheered. "Louie was laid out." He made a sweeping gesture. "Rumor went around that he was laid to rest." Calzone grabbed a daisy out of a vase and held it over his chest. "Now we know the truth. While we strain our brains here in school, Louie Twitwhistle lounges around in a funny nightgown. Pretty nurses are waiting on him hand and foot. He's probably ordering room service right this minute." Calzone sat up on the table. He crossed his arms, leaned backward against the wall and declared, "Louie Twitwhistle is my kind of a guy. He's laid back." Calzone's mouth closed over his teeth and his lips formed a satisfied "Louie" smile.

9 Wishing Him Well

Kara found it hard to get back to work. Between the fire drill and waiting for news about Louie, this had been a stressful and confusing day. Every time she started to concentrate, someone stopped by to put a card for Louie on his desk. By morning recess, almost everyone in the room had designed a special get well card.

Kara still had not made a card. "What would I say?" she wondered.

She picked up one of the homemade cards. It was from Marsha Truffle. "Get well!" announced a plump penguin in battle fatigues. Inside, a picture showed a thin, sickly penguin lying in a hammock on a South Pacific island. There was a big bump on his head and five stars formed the stitches. A bright sun beat down. In Marsha's best handwriting, a message said, "It's not cool to be sick." Then she added a note, "I miss you. Recess won't be the same." She signed it, "Captain Truffle."

Kara opened a card from Ali. "Forget about eating healthy food at the hospital," said the caption on the front. Inside he had drawn a picture of three slugs eating powdered sugar doughnuts and drinking coffee. They were wearing head phones and listening to music. Their names were on their shirts. Their names were Calcium Proprionate, Sulfiting Agent, and Trisodium Phosphate. The caption said, "Preserve yourself!"

Rick drew a banana slug wearing thick glasses. She looked exactly like Ms. Kraut. "Come on Louie," the slug said. "Even I can see that you're faking it."

Kara almost wished she hadn't read the other cards. She was confused about her feelings toward

Louie. She didn't know what to write and she certainly couldn't think of anything clever.

"I hope you'll soon be back to normal," she wrote on a fresh card. But her mind said, "There's always a first time for everything." She tore it up. "I have until Friday to think of an idea. This could be a long week."

Word spread that Louie was in the hospital. Cards began arriving from all over the school. Mrs. Butterhorn got tired of the interruptions, so she put up a sign with a big arrow. It said, "Louie's Place--This Way!"

By Friday morning, Louie's area was overflowing with cards and letters. The pile of cards had spilled over Louie's desk and was forming a large mountain around Kara's desk. She had to take an alternate route to her seat. Besides the cards and letters, several students brought helium balloons. There were butterflies, fish, rainbows, and even a stand-up penguin. Mrs. Jensen ordered a balloon bouquet that threatened to lift the desk right off the floor. The office staff sent a bouquet of flowers with a strong scent that made Kara's nose twitch. Mr. Calzone delivered a large green and white box with a huge bow.

Mrs. Butterhorn made an announcement. "I received word last night that Louie had surgery. He is much better now. The doctor put a metal plate in his head." This sparked a lot of discussion. Mrs. Butterhorn tried her best to explain the surgical procedure.

Ali wasn't listening. He drew a picture of Louie with a plate full of vegetables sticking out of his forehead. He added the picture to the heap of stuff on Louie's desk. It upset the delicate balance and sent cards and letters flying.

"Mrs. Butterhorn," sighed Kara. "May I organize this mess?"

"Why of course," said Mrs. Butterhorn. "That would be very helpful."

Kara looked at the mountain of cards. "I'll need some paper bags and rubber bands," she announced.

"Suit yourself," smiled Mrs. Butterhorn.

Kara set to work, sorting the cards by size and shape and putting them in piles of ten. Then she secured them with rubber bands. She counted 650 cards, plus Ali's picture. After putting the cards into paper bags, she lined the bags up along the door and attached felt pens as weights to each helium balloon. The balloon bouquet had a mind of its own, but she managed to lodge it between a cabinet and Calzone's gift.

She sat and leaned back against her chair, taking a deep breath. Then she put her head down on her desk. As she did so, she looked over at Louie's place. She was proud of the clean desk top. She looked on the floor at Louie's faded blue duffle bag. The small brown trail was gone. She thought about Louie. "He makes me crazy. He's messy and unpredictable. His nose has been running since kindergarten. Yet, somehow I miss him. Maybe it's like the feeling you get when a headache stops, or school's out for the summer.

Why can't I come up with a simple card? Why am I making this so difficult?"

Then an idea popped into her head. Her hand shot up. "Mrs. Butterhorn," she blurted out. "May I look for something in Louie's desk?"

Mrs. Butterhorn looked up from her work. A neat little row of paper bags and balloons lined the room. Louie's desk top shone. She smiled in appreciation.

"Of course, Kara. Anything you want. Thanks for your help."

Kara rummaged through Louie's desk. Books, papers, pencils, and an assortment of junk landed on the floor. Kara didn't seem to notice. A smile spread across her face as she found what she was looking for. She pulled out a large sheet of construction paper. She smoothed out the wrinkles. "This is a mess. I'll need to redo it." She recopied Louie's poster, advertising the Alzheimer's project, on a clean sheet of paper. At the bottom of the poster she added, "Please see

Kara Suko. She's organizing this project for Louie." Then she got out a fresh sheet of lined paper. On it she wrote:

Dear Louie:

I am sorry about your accident. Since you will be out of school for a month, I will organize your Alzheimer's project. It will be no problem at all. You can thank me later. Get well soon!

Sincerely,

Kara Suko

Smiling, she stuffed everything back into Louie's desk and signed out to go to the bathroom.

On her way out the door, she dropped her letter in a paper bag. Once outside, she posted Louie's sign on the bulletin board in the hall. Then she went to the rest room, because Kara Suko always followed the rules.

10 Hats-Off to Louie

The month passed quickly. Louie's desk filled up again. This time it was covered with offers to help with the Alzheimer's project. Again Kara found herself binding notes in piles of tens. She counted notes to volunteer, letters to patients, and stacks of children's art work. There were more helium balloons with cheerful messages of friendship, simple craft projects, rubber stamps, flowering plants, and bird house kits. Kara really had to manage her time to get all her school work done and still organize Louie's project.

Today, Kara was nervous. Today was the date she had set for the visit to Snug Harbor. Mrs. Butterhorn had scheduled the bus. Still, Louie had not returned to school. Organizing the event was one thing, but going ahead without Louie was unthinkable. After all, this was his project. Kara wasn't even sure she could go through with it. She had agreed to work in the gift shop. Now she would be working right with the patients. Kara was scared.

Mrs. Butterhorn had developed a theme around the Alzheimer's project. The students learned to spell "Alzheimer's," explored the anatomy of the brain, and studied the effects of the disease on the patients. Kara found out that people with Alzheimer's can be discipline problems. Sometimes they hit or bite. People exclude them from parties, because they make loud noises and eat the napkins. Some of them have disgusting habits like blowing their noses without tissue. As the disease progresses, many of them wear diapers.

As she sat at her desk stewing about what to do, she heard a bunch of noise in the hall. It sounded like someone singing. She peeked out the door to see what all the excitement was about. Down the hall came a crowd of kids. They were singing "Louie, Louie," and cheering loudly. "Louie lives. Long-Live-Louie!" Above the crowd, she saw a bright green and white form. Why, it looked like the uniform for the Harmony Harbor High School football team. There were the cleats, the green pants, and the white shirt with the number 09. Under the green helmet, wearing a "no-teeth-showing grin", peeked Louie Twitwhistle. Louie, who never played sports, who never wore matching clothes, who never did anything like anyone else, had arrived wearing the Harmony Harbor High School football uniform. He carried a large green and white box in his arms. The crowd lowered Louie to the ground. He headed toward Calzone's room clutching the box.

Kara followed him as he entered Calzone's room. He plunked the box down beside Calzone's desk. Calzone barked his familiar, "Hey, what's happenin'?"

"I came to say 'thanks' and to return your box." He collected thirty new stares in his fashionable helmet and matching accessories.

"Glad you're back Louie," someone called out.

Her curiosity satisfied for the moment, Kara hurried to class.

The students weren't ready to work. They all wanted to hear about Louie's stay in the hospital. Louie described his operation in full detail. He dragged out his x-rays and before-and-after photos. "I have to wear this protective helmet for a while," he explained. "Thank you for sharing," said Mrs. Butterhorn, whose face had turned as green as the helmet.

Kara raised her hand. "May I have some time to bring Louie up-to-date on the Alzheimer's project."

"You may talk quietly, but the rest of us need to start our school work."

"The bus will be here at 3:30 today to take us to Snug Harbor," Kara whispered.

"Today?" said Louie.

"Yes, everything is set. I have thirty volunteers lined up for this first visit. Several teachers have volunteered to go along, including Mr. Calzone and Mrs. Butterhorn. I have organized the activities. Louie listened in awe as Kara described the preparations that she had made. He didn't make any jokes or tease. He didn't even wipe his nose. Louie just stared long and hard at Kara Suko. It was as though he'd never seen her before.

The volunteers created quite a spectacle as they paraded into Snug Harbor Nursing Home. Smiling faces peeked out behind packages filled with crafts and goodies. Lively balloons bobbed and swayed, providing cover for the tiny elves, as they smuggled their surprises into the nursing home. Louie led the procession in his green and white football uniform. At his side was Kara Suko, holding a large bouquet of flowers. Behind the parade of balloons came Mr. Calzone carrying the green and white box.

Louie led the procession.

Once inside the recreation hall, the kids took their places to sing songs that the music teacher, Melody Vanderflute, had taught them. Louie didn't know the words, but he smiled and hummed along. Some residents called out. Others joined in.

When they finished, the kids each found a resident to work with. They painted, and built bird houses. Ole Olsen teased Ali and Rick by barking at them and making other threatening noises. "Ole hasn't been this alert in weeks!" remarked a nurse.

Julienne Beane curled up on the easy chair with Esther Samuelson. "I'm sleepy and I want to go to bed," Esther pleaded. They cuddled. Lucy Goodwin, a former secretary, stamped documents with rubber stamps, and Angie Haines painted with water colors. The kids read books, and the patients rolled play dough. Tom Gills, who raised fifty-two foster children, tried to control a bouquet of helium balloons. A tiny smile turned up the corner of his mouth.

The nurses made sure no one left the room or acted out. The residents talked and sang. Smiling and nodding, they ate homemade muffins and finger-Jello. Decorating a gingerbread house was a big hit. No one seemed to notice that it was a little out of season.

The children got out the hat box and everyone put on a hat. Ali's hat had an alligator on it. Rick wore a beanie with a propeller. Kara chose a crown. Soon all the residents and kids were wearing silly hats. Louie spotted a hat with sunglasses, a hat with clapping hands, a frog hat, and a sombrero. Mrs. Butterhorn wore a hat with an umbrella. For once, even Mrs. Butterhorn could see hats.

Everyone was wearing a silly hat.

The children seated the patients around a long table that was made by pushing several tables together. Everyone played beach ball and laughed at the funny hats.

The beach ball bounced toward Calzone. Suddenly, the kids noticed that Calzone's head was bare. "Where's your hat?" asked Louie. Mr. Calzone had been waiting for this moment. "Let's have a drum roll," he called. He began to pound the table with his pointer fingers. Soon everyone joined in. It made a great sound. "Ta ta da," Calzone sang as he reached into the box. He took out his hat and plunked it on his head. All eyes were on Calzone, as he adjusted the French helmet for comfort. A note fell out onto the table.

"What's it say?" Sam Sakamoto shouted.

Calzone read aloud, "Thanks for the new helmet. I won't be needing this one anymore. Ms. Kraut says it simply won't do in middle school. She says I need to conform to standards, blend in a little more. Besides, thanks to a flying bat and the miracles of medicine I'll always be the real Metal Head. I'd like you to have my helmet." The note was signed, Louie Twitwhistle, Ph. D. (Phenomenal Dude).

"Mercy bow-coop," said Calzone. "That's English for merci beaucoup," he smiled.

Everyone laughed. "What's that sound?" asked Louie.

As the giggling stopped, a male voice could be heard singing, first gently and then louder. Louie looked around to see where the sound was coming from. The tune was familiar. The music was coming from a white-haired gentleman seated in the corner. His legs were crossed and he was swinging his right leg to the music. Louie's eyes followed the long, bobbing, blue slipper.

"I'd know that huge foot anywhere," Louie thought. "It's L. Edwards, the World War I veteran."

Mr. Edwards continued to sing the theme song from the war. "Over there. Over there. Send the word, send the word over there."

Louie hadn't met Mr. Edwards, but he'd read
his biography.

> L. Edwards served in the 42nd
> Division, nicknamed the Rainbow
> Division, commanded by Major
> MacArthur. He served as a runner
> or messenger between the troops in
> France. He survived a gas attack
> and earned the purple heart.

The French helmet had magically sparked a
memory. As Mr. Edwards sang, he fingered a
metal tag that hung from his neck. Louie strained
to read, "#100321." Mr. Edwards turned the
silver disk over. "PVT 1CL C 168. Private First
Class--Company 168," Louie decoded.

Then Louie began to lecture in a serious
tone. "World War I--Woodrow Wilson called it
'the war to end all wars.' Too bad it didn't.
World War I established the rights of small nations
to make their own rules and to navigate in open

seas. The world stopped a powerful bully, who wanted everybody to do things his way."

Louie had his own war going on. He was a nation unto himself. "I won't give up the fight," he thought. "Middle school might require some new strategies, but I'll always be myself. After all, there's only one Louie Twitwhistle," he lectured to an internal audience.

Louie walked over to Calzone. He whispered something in his ear. Calzone removed the French helmet from his head and handed it to Louie. Louie went to Mr. Edwards and placed the helmet on his head. Mr. Edwards smiled a big wide smile. "Thank you," he whispered.

"I'll find you another one," he called to Calzone. "The French made thousands of them. I'm sure they have one or two left over." Calzone didn't answer. He seemed to have something in his eye.

Turning his attention back to Mr. Edwards, Louie asked, "By the way, what does the L. in your name stand for?"

Mr. Edwards' answer came in a hoarse whisper. "My name is Louis, pronounced 'Louie' like the French kings."

At that moment, Mrs. Clearview arrived with an announcement. "Your bus is here. Everything ran smoothly and the nursing staff wants to thank you."

"Hats-off to Louie!" called Ali Abrams. At that a few kids began to throw their hats into the air. Soon everyone was throwing hats and cheering.

Everyone threw hats and cheered.

Everyone, that is, except Louie. He was staring at Mr. Edwards. He gave Mr. Edwards a quick salute and turned to go. "I'll save you, 'Left-Over Louie,'" he mouthed, as a single tear rolled down his face.

"Speech! Speech!" someone called.

Louie fidgeted and rolled his shoulders back and forth. He rubbed the football helmet. "He's thinking," someone whispered.

"This would not have been possible without Kara Suko," said Louie. "I had the idea, but she organized the whole thing."

"It was nothing," said Kara. "Anyone could have done it."

"Maybe," said Louie, "but you did it."

Kara's mouth slowly opened into a wide smile. Louie, the master stare collector, gazed at Kara as if he were seeing her for the first time. As their eyes met, he gathered thirty gawks. Then Louie did something no one had ever seen him do before. Louie Twitwhistle blushed.

THE END

Epilogue

*S*o there you have it. I had a new "best seller," and Mrs. Butterhorn's class became famous. Their pictures appeared in the local newspapers, and Channel 8 declared Mrs. Butterhorn "Teacher of the Year." At a school assembly Mr. Gritz presented her with the "Apple of My Eye Award," and in her honor he made a new school rule, "ALWAYS BE YOURSELF." Then Mr. Gritz did several things nobody had ever seen him do before. John Duane Gritz tipped his ten gallon hat, gave a little bow, and winked at Mrs. Butterhorn.

The author

ORDERING INFORMATION

To order additional copies, send check or money order to
Gig Harbor Press
P.O. Box 2059A
Gig Harbor, WA 98335
for:

Left-Over Louie 1-883078-76-8 @ $11.95

Sales Tax:
Add 7.8% for books shipped to Washington addresses

Shipping:
Book Rate: Add $2.00 for the first book and 75 cents
for each additional book. (Allow 3 - 6 weeks)

**Be sure to include your name, mailing address and the
number of copies requested.**